"Dance with me."

Those dark eyes stared back at him. He wanted to rip that mask off and see her entire face, but part of him liked this allure. And maybe Delilah liked it, too. She hadn't walked away and she hadn't said no.

"Cam."

He took her clutch from beneath her arm and escorted her toward the dance floor, stopping long enough at his table to set her purse down. She didn't hesitate, but he knew her mind and she was running through all the reasons why this was a bad decision. Well, he was going through all the reasons why this was the *best* decision.

With an expert move, Camden spun her around and gave a slight tug until she fell against his chest. Her hands clamped around his shoulders, her delicate touch nearly singed through his thin shirt.

"We shouldn't do this," she murmured, but made no motion to pull away.

* * *

Second Chance Vows by Jules Bennett
is part of the Angel's Share series.

Dear Reader,

Welcome to book two of my Angel's Share series! I hope you are just as excited as I am to revisit Benton Springs and this old castle-turned-distillery. Who doesn't love kick-ass women dominating a man's world? Up next is the sister who experienced some heartache in *When the Lights Go Out*...

You might recall Delilah was on the verge of divorce, but Camden has other plans for her. No way is he admitting defeat in any aspect of his life—especially not his marriage.

You have no idea how excited I get when I can reconnect a couple! I love seeing them break, then realize they need each other to rebuild. Sometimes in life, it's okay to admit you need help and that can actually make you stronger. Cam and Delilah desperately need each other, though they are both much too stubborn to admit such a thing.

I hope you enjoy this romance full of rekindling, passion and drama. Be sure to stay tuned for Sara's story coming up next! I've got something special planned for her...

Happy reading,

Jules

JULES BENNETT

—

SECOND CHANCE VOWS

HARLEQUIN®
DESIRE™

Recycling programs for this product may not exist in your area.

ISBN-13: 978-1-335-58135-8

Second Chance Vows

Harlequin Enterprises ULC
22 Adelaide St. West, 41st Floor
Toronto, Ontario M5H 4E3, Canada
www.Harlequin.com

Printed in U.S.A.

USA TODAY bestselling author **Jules Bennett** has published over sixty books and never tires of writing happy endings. Writing strong heroines and alpha heroes is Jules's favorite way to spend her workdays. Jules hosts weekly contests on her Facebook fan page and loves chatting with readers on Twitter, Facebook and via email through her website. Stay up-to-date by signing up for her newsletter at julesbennett.com.

Books by Jules Bennett

Harlequin Desire

The Rancher's Heirs

Twin Secrets
Claimed by the Rancher
Taming the Texan
A Texan for Christmas

Lockwood Lightning

An Unexpected Scandal
Scandalous Reunion
Scandalous Engagement

Angel's Share

When the Lights Go Out...
Second Chance Vows

Visit her Author Profile page at Harlequin.com, or julesbennett.com, for more titles.

You can also find Jules Bennett on Facebook, along with other Harlequin Desire authors, at Facebook.com/harlequindesireauthors!

To all my loyal readers—thank you for making my dreams come true.

One

This corset was much too tight, but seeing as how she was already at the party, there was no going back.

Unfortunately, the ill-fitting costume was the least of Delilah Preston's worries tonight. Why had she agreed to meet a guy blindly? Her divorce wasn't final, but Alisha Martin had been so persuasive and wouldn't take no for an answer.

Which is how Delilah found herself dressed all in black from her eye mask, to her corset and leather pants, and stilettos. She'd even donned black nail polish for the event. She hadn't wanted to invest in a new costume she'd likely never wear again, so going as a shadow seemed fun—or at least the most fun she was ready to have at this stage in her life. Maybe she could simply sneak out when she was ready to leave. She hadn't exactly been in a partying mood over the past several months.

Having a marriage crumble into a pile of unrecognizable pieces would do that.

But, this was her first outing in a month and she had to do something about her lack of social life or she'd drive herself insane. Staying home binge-watching one series after another only grew more depressing by the day.

Alisha Martin was a new client to Angel's Share, the bourbon distillery Delilah owned with her sisters. Elise, Sara and Dee had started their distillery journey over a decade ago when they'd purchased the old castle in the heart of bourbon country. The impressive stone structure had been a teen hangout back in the day, but when the sisters decided to get serious about opening a distillery, they knew they needed something unique to set them apart in this man's world. What better place than an abandoned castle?

And the name had been easy for them. When bourbon went into a barrel to age, some of the liquid evaporated and the old saying was that the portion missing was sent to the angels.

Delilah loved everything about this world they'd created. Not to mention they'd met so many amazing people through the years. They'd secured a solid client base and they'd also made some great friendships through their connections.

Alisha had been to the distillery several times over the past month to get a variety of bourbons and gin supplied for her charity event, Home Sweeter Home. She was such a giving, caring person that when Alisha insisted Delilah show up for this costume party for the children's orphanage, Dee couldn't say no.

Then Alisha had texted last minute to say there was a really nice guy Delilah should meet who would also be at the party. In that instant, Dee wasn't so afraid of saying no, but her reply had gone unanswered.

Okay. All she had to do was go in, see Alisha, make her donation and slink out. The all-black shadow costume would be perfect for this stealth mission. She really should have sent Sara or Elise in her place, but her sisters were busy leading their own lives. Good for them. At least two-thirds of her tight circle had something to look forward to.

Delilah pulled in a deep breath and headed up the concrete steps that led to the double glass doors of The Grandeur, a historic mansion turned event space. The greeters opened the doors to let her in and she offered them each a smile.

As soon as she stepped inside, the music, laughter and chatter hit her all at once. This wasn't something she was cut out for. She liked things nice and quiet in her office where she could focus on the business and her new clients. She enjoyed a relaxed atmosphere and serenity. She thrived on peace, which was ironic considering her life lately was anything but peaceful.

What she did not enjoy was the boning on this corset. The damn thing had fit last year. Must have shrunk in her drawer.

Resisting the urge to adjust her costume, Delilah made her way into the ballroom and glanced around at the sea of people. She should have asked what Alisha was going to be dressed as. It could take a while to find her considering nearly everyone wore a mask.

Having a good portion of her face covered was a good thing, though, because there wasn't a doubt in her mind that her pretentious in-laws would be here.

Correction—soon-to-be former in-laws. If there was a way for them to shove their name and money in front of people, they were first through the door…which was why they certainly did not like it when their only child married a girl who had been adopted and came from humble beginnings.

Delilah tucked her black clutch beneath her arm and wove her way through the crowds of people milling about. She assumed if she headed toward the stage at the front of the ballroom, maybe Alisha would be there and Dee could slip her the donation quick and easy. Then she could escape as stealthily as she'd come in and there would be no run-ins with Camden's parents, no introduction to this mystery man that Alisha had set up for her.

"Delilah?"

She spun around at the familiar voice and forced a smile. "Alisha."

Her client and new friend was stunning in her white-and-gold goddess costume. With her flowing blond hair and striking green eyes, she looked absolutely flawless, like an actress from a movie set.

"I thought that was you," Alisha stated as she moved closer. "I don't know what your costume is, but I'm jealous of how gorgeous and fit you are."

Delilah laughed. "I'm a shadow and believe me, this costume is holding in all the rolls. I'm not actually this curvy."

More like frumpy. Some people lost weight during a breakup, but Delilah seemed to be finding the pounds. She couldn't help that angel food cake with extra whip had been bringing her comfort over the past several months.

"Well, regardless, I'm so glad you could come," Alisha went on. "I just spoke with the guy I was telling you about. He arrived right before you did, so this is perfect timing."

Delilah cringed. "I appreciate you wanting to

play Cupid, but I'm not really in a position to meet anyone new. I'm actually not even divorced yet."

Alisha placed a hand on Dee's shoulder. "That's ironic you say that because he just told me the same thing. Listen, he's super nice, so maybe he'd be a good friend to have since you're both going through the same ordeal. Sometimes talking to a stranger is therapeutic."

Maybe so. The only people who really knew her situation were her sisters. Delilah didn't like failure, never wanted to believe that her marriage was over, but she and Camden weren't on the same page anymore and attraction and chemistry would only carry them so far.

Alisha smoothed her hair away from her face and Delilah caught a glimpse of an impressive rock on her very important finger.

"Is that new?" Delilah asked, reached for her hand. "It's gorgeous."

Alisha beamed. "It is. I just got back from a little impromptu vacation that took quite a different turn than I was expecting."

"Sounds intriguing." Delilah released her hand and smiled. "I look forward to hearing about it when you're free."

"It's quite a story." Alisha smiled. "We'll do lunch soon and I'll tell you all about it."

Love literally seemed to be surrounding De-lilah. No matter where she went. She was truly happy for all of these people in her life. She just wished her own marriage hadn't turned into such a heartbreaking mess.

"Oh, here he comes now." Alisha's eyes landed over Delilah's shoulder as she smiled and waved at someone. "He's the one dressed as a pirate with the eye patch."

Delilah glanced around and spotted the stranger Alisha described. The sexy man with tight black pants and a billowy white shirt, dark scruff along his square jawline, one deep brown eye staring back at her was no stranger at all.

This was her husband.

Camden was coming to tell Alisha that he was going to skip out and to thank her for the invite. He definitely wasn't up for meeting anyone new although he'd thought he was ready to socialize, but the instant he'd gotten here, that proved to be wrong. His parents were thankfully out of town so at least he hadn't had to deal with that face-to-face encounter. Dodging their phone calls was more than enough of a workout without adding a social event to the mix.

He shifted his focus to the event host across the room and made his way toward her. Alisha stood next to a woman dressed in all black with a black mask over her eyes. Oh, hell...

She might be trying to disguise herself so nobody would know who she was, but he knew. Camden knew every dip and curve of that body as he'd lain beside it for the past five years.

"Delilah, this is Camden, the guy I was telling you about."

Cam waited for Alisha to finish the introduction before he reached out his hand. "It's a pleasure."

Dee's mouth opened wide and he couldn't help but smile as she placed her hand in his. That spark of chemistry and awareness never got old, never fizzled out. Their attraction had always been high and hot. If sex alone could keep a marriage together, they wouldn't be in the situation they were now.

But their jobs, his family and lack of communication were leading them down a path he never thought he'd be taking.

Camden wanted his wife back. He'd made no secret about that, but Delilah claimed she had put up with enough and she didn't see them moving forward in a direction she needed to go. They couldn't get their futures on the same page and for that reason alone, she'd asked him to file the divorce papers, which he did reluctantly.

The irony that he did this for a living didn't escape him. He was a divorce attorney who never thought his firm would be working on his own case.

"Oh, excuse me," Alisha added. "The caterer is motioning for me."

As soon as she stepped away, Delilah separated their bond and clasped her hands together. He didn't know if she was trying to rub away his touch or secretly hold on to it. Either way, he had an effect on her and she sure as hell had a hold over him. All of this damn baggage that they'd carried for years had finally broken both of them. Failure had never been an option for him and he certainly didn't like that feeling now.

Being a divorce lawyer and having his own marriage fail seemed like such a slap in the face. This was not the life he'd envisioned or worked so hard to achieve.

"What are you doing here?" she whispered as she leaned in closer.

"Alisha is the sister of the newest guy at our firm," he told her. "How do you know her?"

Delilah pointed at a server walking around with a tray of tumblers and cocktails. "She's using Angel's Share spirits tonight."

"Where are Sara and Elise?" he asked.

"My sisters were both busy tonight so I had to make an appearance."

And he was sure that pissed her off. His Delilah was quiet and much preferred staying behind the scenes. She kept her head down and her drive high. The woman was passionate about every aspect of her life from her work to their marriage… and he hadn't appreciated her when he'd had her.

The music switched from upbeat to something more soothing and slow with a sultry beat...but of course. Just one more thing mocking him and this entire situation.

Camden took in her body-hugging outfit and the half mask that left her red lips exposed...and way too damn tempting. He'd always loved the contrast of her dark skin with red lipstick. She knew it, too. Any time they'd gone out, she'd always put on his favorite shade—the exact one she was wearing now.

That made him wonder how many other times she'd worn it since they separated and she moved out of their home.

Her moving out and leaving the house to him had been yet another bone of contention between them.

Camden reached for her and settled his hand right in the dip at her waist. She stilled beneath him and he cursed himself for ever allowing their relationship to get to the point his own wife questioned his touch.

"Dance with me."

Those dark eyes stared back at him. He wanted to rip her mask off and see her entire face, but part of him liked this allure. And maybe she liked it, too. She hadn't walked away and she hadn't said no, so that was at least a step up from their last encounter when he'd kissed her in a back room during another very public event. He hadn't seen her since the gala at Angel's Share celebrating the launch of their ten-year bourbon, so they hadn't talked about the private moment.

"Cam."

He took her clutch from beneath her arm and escorted her toward the dance floor, stopping long enough at his table to set her purse down. She didn't hesitate, but he knew her mind and she was running through all the reasons this was a bad decision. Well, he was going through all the reasons this was the best decision.

With an expert move, Camden spun her around and gave a slight tug until she fell against his chest. Her hands clamped around his shoulders, and her delicate touch nearly singed through his thin shirt.

"We shouldn't do this," she murmured, but made no motion to pull away.

Camden started swaying with her body moving perfectly against his. She wouldn't cause a scene, not here. She might want to run like she did at the Angel's Share gala last month, but that had been a little easier for her to escape from.

"Why is that?" he whispered as he leaned in closer. "Because you're afraid?"

"I'm not afraid of anything."

"No? Then why haven't you returned my texts since the kiss?"

Her eyes darted down and they both knew he'd

just made a solid point. Which was pretty much his job, but he never once wanted to use his career skills on his own wife. He wanted them to be a team; he'd wanted her to be his forever.

But she'd started wanting more than he thought he could give. A high-profile career demanded most of his time and she fell further and further back in his life. Added to that, his parents had always been an invisible wedge between them. Whenever they could, they made a special point to leave veiled hints that Delilah's social background didn't match theirs. He shrugged it off, but Cam didn't realize Dee took it to heart.

For years all of those differences festered and grew, until one day Dee had simply had enough. If they were together too long, those differences between them would rise back up into an argument and the cycle would start all over again.

He wanted to break that series of unpleasant patterns they found themselves locked in. He had no idea how, but he had to make her see that they belonged together. He never lost anything in his life and he sure as hell wasn't about to start with his wife.

"That kiss was a mistake," she told him between gritted teeth.

"Didn't feel like a mistake." Camden slid his hand to the small of her back and held her closer. "It felt like you wanted more."

Her eyes snapped to his. "What I want and what I can have are two very different realities."

So she did want him. He knew that part of their relationship would never die no matter what. Now if he could figure out how to bridge her wants and her needs and stay true to his own needs, they'd be back on a level playing field.

Maybe that's all they needed—to get back to the basics. Maybe they should start over and lay a solid foundation first. Every moment of their lives together had been hectic and rushed, what with his schedule and traveling all over to his high-profile clientele as he started his own firm to her building up Angel's Share with her best friends who were also her adopted sisters. He was damn proud of her and all she'd accomplished. Maybe he hadn't shown her or taken the extra time to tell her.

How the hell could he turn this marriage from a loss to a win?

"There's nothing wrong with giving into your desires." He shifted back to the moment and the woman in his arms…exactly where she should be. "We're both adults who want each other."

"It's not right," she declared.

Camden spun her around, slowly maneuvering her closer to one of the tables his firm had sponsored. Having her admit out loud she wanted him seemed like a victory he should celebrate and hone in on. There could be no room for negativity, not if he wanted to move forward with her.

"What's wrong is ignoring each other because when we get too close, we want to tear our clothes off."

Delilah went still beneath him and he stopped, too. Her eyes continued to hold his gaze and he knew what she was thinking. They'd been married for five years and there was no way she could lie to him...or to herself.

Camden knew she had so many thoughts rolling through her mind. There wasn't a doubt that right now she was contemplating what it would be like to sleep with him again. Would it be worth the risk? Would they fall back into old habits and still have a broken marriage?

At this point, he just wanted tonight. He just wanted his wife back in his bed. He'd worry about the rest tomorrow. He'd been without her for too damn long and that kiss last month, coupled with the leather pants, tight corset that did amazing things to her breasts, and her soft red lips, had pushed him way too far.

That was the crux of the problem. There was never *enough* Delilah and that's what scared him the most. Even after the years they'd spent together, there was always more of a need that he simply could not control.

"You're still the sexiest woman I've ever

known," he added. "One night. We don't have to think about or even discuss the divorce or anything else."

She closed her eyes and pulled in a deep breath. "That's how we got into this mess, Cam. When we only give in to our desires and don't care about the consequences or the reality surrounding us and working against us."

"What consequences? And the reality is, we already filed for divorce. Neither of us has expectations. It's one night, Dee. Your place or mine. Wherever you want."

When her lids fluttered open, there was that familiar passion staring back at him.

He had her. They'd never been able to deny each other. Their physical intimacy was unlike anything he'd ever had before and he knew if he lost her for good, he'd never find this again.

Camden's body stirred and they were going to have to leave before he made a scene by giving his wife a proper kiss and figuring out how the hell this corset thing worked. He'd seen this piece in their closet a few times and always wondered when she'd wear it…he'd always hoped for a private showing.

"My place," she told him. "I can't go back…"

Home. The word hovered between them just the same as if she'd said it. When she decided they had to separate, he'd told her he would go, but she said she needed a new start without the memories.

That was another revealing sign that she still loved him. Staying in the house he'd purchased before they got married would only remind her of all the things they'd shared within those walls. Hell, he lived through it every single day, but he tried to keep busy and stay out of the home as much as possible for that very reason.

As much as Delilah wanted to erase him in her attempt to move on, he wasn't about to let that happen. They'd started off so hot for each other, skipped a good bit of the get-to-know-you phase and headed down the aisle. Sure, they'd rushed things, but did that make their relationship wrong or a failure? He refused to believe any of that.

Had he filed the divorce papers? Yes. Did he have regrets? Hell, yes.

His parents had accused her of looking for easy money and help with her business venture, but they didn't know Delilah. She never took a dollar from him to help with the progress and growth of Angel's Share. She was too proud and too headstrong to take handouts and he admired her for that…even if her determination could be frustrating at times.

He'd played the middleman for years between his family and his wife. Delilah had apologized, thinking she'd been the catalyst that had driven them apart, but all she did was open his eyes to the controlling, shallow people who had raised him.

Now that they were split up, Camden was even more protective. Delilah was still in such a vulnerable position with their marriage crumbling and Milly passing away. The woman had raised Dee and her sisters and she'd been the only mother they'd known. Suffering such a devastating loss after separating from Cam hadn't put Delilah in a position to put too much into fighting for their marriage. She was emotionally drained and exhausted from the hurt and pain she lived with daily.

The divorce wasn't official, but the clock was ticking. The final papers would be in any day and then he'd have to face the reality that she could be lost forever…which also meant he'd be losing. He'd been lucky that the first time the papers had been filed, there had been some things that weren't right, so they'd had to refile. Thankfully he'd caught the mistake before signing.

But Camden hadn't been lying. He wasn't going to think of anything but tonight.

He gripped her hand, grabbed her clutch off the table and found the nearest exit.

Two

What did she think she was doing?

Avoiding her soon-to-be ex was the only way Delilah was ever going to get over him. So how did she find herself cozied up in the front seat of his SUV?

Letting him lead her from that overly crowded party had seemed like a good idea, but now red flags started waving around in her head and she really should start paying attention to them.

Being reckless is what got her caught up in a marriage built on a crumbling foundation.

"Don't start thinking," he commanded as he maneuvered through town. "I can practically hear your thoughts."

She had no doubt. Camden Preston knew her better than anyone, including her sisters or Milly.

Her *sisters*. That was a whole other area that weighed so heavy on her mind. Finding out her best friends—adoptive sisters—were actually her biological sisters…that life-altering news hit only a few weeks ago and everything was still so fresh.

She hadn't told anyone about what happened. Her first thought had been to run to Camden for support, but those days were over. Seeking a divorce meant severing all ties and starting over.

Yet here she was in his car heading back to her place because the memories of their house would be too much. They'd created a life there. They'd loved, they'd laughed and ultimately, they'd grown apart in the very place she'd thought of as her haven. There were simply too many emotions wrapped into each and every room.

She wanted Cam. Of course she did. Not a day went by since she'd walked out that she hadn't craved his touch or wished she could settle in beside him in their bed. Seeing him at her gala last month had been like another slap to the face, as if she needed the reminder of all she'd lost.

When Cam had asked to speak to her privately, they'd slipped into the back room and he'd kissed her. No words, no touching. He'd backed her against the wall and covered her mouth with his as his body, so perfectly aligned with her own, pressed against her...and she'd thought of little else since.

The man had always been potent. He'd always been able to turn her on with just a look, but kissing her without touching her anywhere else had nearly had her begging right there in a back room, mere steps away from two hundred guests at the black-tie affair she and her sisters hosted.

"Relax."

Camden reached for her hand just like he had countless times before...but this night was different. This night they weren't together, they were still on opposite sides of that invisible line that had been drawn between them. They were each too stubborn and driven to cross over and compromise.

But some things, like careers and family, couldn't be compromised. No matter their feelings for each other, there were still very real issues at hand. Camden had mentioned children about a year ago and that was definitely something they should have discussed before marriage because he wanted them and she hadn't thought much about it. That was the least of their issues, though. His horrid parents and that damn schedule of his kept them torn apart without bringing children into the mix.

"Wanting each other doesn't have to mean more than just that."

Camden stroked the back of her hand with his

thumb, pulling her from their differences and problems and back to the fact her body was heating up just like it always did with this man. His strength and warmth had always been major turn-ons and now, after being without him for seven months, she was barely holding on to her self-control.

Delilah couldn't even concentrate on what he was saying, not when every part of her was revved up. Her desire and need trumped all of those glaring warnings she should be paying attention to.

"Don't talk," she told him. "Just…drive."

If he kept talking, she'd keep thinking, and if she kept thinking, she'd talk herself out of going back to her new place with him…because the unspoken intentions were extremely clear. Sex was all that could be on the table tonight. Not their differences, not their divorce and not all of the very real emotions that still lived so deeply within them.

But Camden was right. They were both adults. They were still married and just because they'd filed for divorce didn't mean they couldn't be intimate. At least now she knew there were no expectations. She was heading into this night with eyes wide open and knew full well everything this was…and wasn't.

They'd both be temporarily satisfied and right now, that's all she wanted. She'd been without Cam's touch for too long and if she could have a sliver of a distraction, she was going to take it. Maybe this was the closure they both needed.

When Delilah had left their shared home, she knew starting over would be difficult, but she hadn't thought about how she would handle the physical side of losing her husband. And that was just her marriage—the other part of her personal life was falling apart as well. The only thing that seemed to be going right for Delilah was her career.

Angel's Share was a success and its sales were skyrocketing. They were not only the only female-run distillery in the country, they were surpassing most others, and with their ten-year bourbon now on the market, sales were increasing faster than projected. People came from all over the country, and even outside the US, to see their castle-turned-distillery. They'd tapped into a gold mine and she couldn't be more proud of all she, Elise and Sara had created.

But that's everything she'd wanted, right? She'd wanted to prove she and her sisters could do something no woman had ever done before. She wanted to prove to everyone, and herself, that she was meant to be in this position and she could not only compete in a man's world but also dominate.

She wondered if the cost had been too high, though.

"There is nothing more than this night," she informed him. "There can't be. I can't work backward, Cam."

Her intentions had to be crystal clear. If she'd sacrificed for her career, she couldn't start reliving the past or she'd just keep going in circles and not moving forward like she planned. Everything was planned...except this damn divorce. That had never been part of her life goals.

The distillery had given her that sense of belonging, of acceptance. She'd never fully felt either of those things with Camden and his family. There had always been that invisible wedge between them and there was no erasing that...not as long as his parents were so disapproving.

Camden squeezed her hand and released it. Then he curled his fingers around her inner thigh, setting off all sorts of other bells than just moments ago. When he touched her, all the heavy barriers between them seemed to vanish and everything in her wanted to just take everything she truly desired.

"What costume is this, anyway?" he asked. "Besides sexy as hell."

His hand massaged way too close to that juncture where she ached most. Instinctively, she slid down in her seat. Why did she have to want the one man who didn't have the same vision for the future as she did? How could they be so perfect on so many levels, yet so wrong on others?

"Um… I'm a…a shadow. I wanted to disappear in the crowd. I actually thought your parents would be there."

His hand shifted just enough and cupped her heat, nearly causing her eyes to roll back in her head. He'd always been such a selfless lover, always putting her needs first.

"They're out of town. And disappear?" he asked with a subtle laugh. "Not possible, babe."

Babe. The word slid out as he continued to massage her. His endearments had always been laced with a heavy seductive tone. Her weakness had always been his touch, whether it be simple or a stepping-stone to something more. He'd had a hold over her physically and emotionally that she'd fought to break free from…and clearly she hadn't fought hard enough.

"You're tensing up again," he murmured as he turned into her driveway. "We can't have that."

He stopped the vehicle halfway up the drive beneath a canopy of trees and put it in Park. Moonlight filtered through the minuscule openings between the leaves, casting the gentlest glow into the vehicle.

"What are you doing?" she asked.

Camden didn't answer. Another career skill she knew he carried over into his daily life had always been less talking and more action. It was those nonverbal communications she needed to be worried about. The man was a master at getting his way without using a single word. Then again, she wasn't exactly arguing. How could she when she'd missed this very thing?

He reached over, grasped her face in his hands and pulled her mouth to his, as if he couldn't take another second of being this close and not tasting her.

It had been too damn long. An entire month without his lips, and even longer without his body. Delilah wondered if he fully intended to strip her in the front seat of his car or if they'd actually make it up to the house before she combusted.

Delilah came to life in his arms…just like he'd expected. She might put up a verbal fight, but she wanted the same things he did—physically, anyway. Emotionally, they weren't on the same level. Yet.

But Camden wasn't here for the emotional aspect. He wanted his wife and he knew full well she wanted him, too. This separation between them had gone on too long.

Delilah shifted in her seat, then brought one hand up to the side of his face. His beard scraped against her hand, a sound he always loved. She freely opened for him and moaned the moment his tongue swept against hers. His entire body stirred, aching even more than before. There were too many barriers, too many gadgets in the way.

He'd been unable to stop himself like he was some damn teenager without self-control.

Just when he was about to put an end to this madness and take her up to the house and into a bed like she deserved, Delilah pushed him back. For a half second he thought she was putting the brakes on, but then he saw her eyes. There was a hunger staring back that he recognized.

Camden fell back against his seat and Dee started stripping out of her heels and peeled the leather pants down her lean legs. Watching her bare legs work the leather the rest of the way down and finally off nearly had him embarrassing himself.

With the corset still in place, accentuating the fullness of her breasts, Delilah climbed over the center console and straddled his lap. She bumped the horn and jumped, then started laughing.

"I'll scoot my seat back," he muttered as he watched her going to work on the zipper of his dress pants. "Or we could just go on up to the house."

"You started this too early and I can't wait," she panted.

The moment she released him and covered him with her hand, Camden dropped his head back against the seat and groaned. As much as he wanted her in the house where he could fully explore that body he'd missed, he also had gone way too long without his wife's touch.

And knowing she was this on fire wasn't surprising. Delilah had always been a passionate woman. He could read more into this moment, having her wrapped all around him, but he was still realistic. He knew tonight was all about being physical. Delilah wasn't thinking beyond right now…which was just fine with him. He was having a difficult time thinking, too.

Camden filled his hands with bare backside and guided her so her core would replace her hand. His silent gesture had her reaching to grip his shoulders a second before she joined their bodies.

The cry she let out had him gritting his teeth to remain somewhat in control. With Delilah's sweet body working against his and those familiar pants and moans, he was seriously struggling to let her have her way—but he was willing to give her any physical thing she needed.

Cam wanted to touch her more, wanted the rest of their clothes off and not to be in the front seat of his damn car…but right now, he was going to take what he could get because he needed this. They both needed this. And if she needed to keep hold of those reins in this roller-coaster marriage, he wasn't going to argue.

Cutting off their relationship so completely hadn't been right. He didn't want to be that man who couldn't hold his own marriage together and watched it crumble in his hands. The fact that he looked incompetent as a husband would never sit well with him.

But the weight of this heavy failure wasn't something he could focus on right now. He wanted to take in every single euphoric moment with his wife, even if this wasn't exactly how he'd imagined things. He'd rather have her in their home, in their bed...not in the driveway of some rental home she'd found.

Delilah threw her head back as her hips jerked faster. Her body clenched all around him as she ultimately stilled and bit down on her bottom lip, a sure sign she was struggling to maintain her composure. No need to hold back on his account. He wanted her to let go. He needed to see her come undone, to know he was the one who made her feel this way. And he wanted her to know it, too. Camden gripped her hips tighter and held her in place, triggering her release as he let his own climax take over.

Her warm breath tickled the side of his face as she leaned farther into him. Her body trembled, or maybe that was his. Either way, he wasn't ready for this moment to end, despite the fact they were in his car like teenagers. This was his *wife*, damn it. He wanted to ride this high and carry her with him and forget everything else and all the reasons they couldn't make this marriage work.

Carefully, Camden shifted her body slightly and

rested her head on his shoulder. He reached around her and put the car in Drive.

"You're not seriously driving," she murmured against his neck.

"I want you in the bedroom, Dee. Or at least outside of this car. I'm not nearly done."

Her lips grazed his skin and he nearly ran the damn car into the landscaping as he pulled up near the front porch. He couldn't get the car in Park fast enough before he killed the engine and threw open his door.

"I'm glad this place is shielded from your neighbors," he told her as he maneuvered out of the SUV, cupping her backside to keep her against him as he looked over her shoulder.

"Privacy is always important," she muttered. "Go to the garage and use the keypad."

She gave him the code and he was in the garage and had the door going down within seconds. He hadn't been inside her new house and honestly he'd never wanted to be. He'd wanted her to rethink their future together and come back home where she belonged.

Their living arrangements were definitely a conversation for another time.

"I never thought you'd be here."

"That makes two of us." Cam headed toward the door leading into the house. "Where's your bedroom?"

"There's a guest bedroom down here." She pointed without glancing up from the crook of his neck. "First door on the right down that hallway."

A pang of anger hit him as he realized she didn't want him in her bedroom, but he was here and he had to take his own advice. This night wasn't about any attempt to reconcile—he didn't even know if such a thing was possible.

Everything tonight was purely physical. No emotions could or should be involved. Letting all of their feelings intermingle with sex was how they'd fallen so fast and hard with each other and ended up walking into the courthouse for a spur-of-the-moment wedding not long after meeting.

Had they set themselves up for failure from the start?

Maybe so, but he had every intention of changing the outcome and not signing those damn papers.

Camden followed her directions and stepped inside the bedroom. Slowly, he eased her down his body until she came to stand before him. The only light was from the hallway, but it was more than enough for him to take in the sight of his breathtaking wife as she stood before him wearing only a corset. Her hair had come undone and spread all around her shoulders. Her red lipstick had worn off, but those eyes were still heavily made-up, which gave her even more of that vixen aura.

That was his Delilah. She could be anything

from sexy siren to sweet seductress. He'd loved both, but apparently that hadn't been enough. Sex and love didn't hold a marriage together. Her goals hadn't aligned with his and they'd both been shocked to find out how the other saw their future together because nothing was remotely the same.

He'd mentioned family and she hadn't really thought much past her career. He'd thought maybe she'd slow down with that, but she was just getting started. Not that he didn't value her job. He just hadn't wanted her to feel like she had to have such a demanding career.

Throw into the mix his disapproving family and the entire situation went all to hell.

Damn it. Why couldn't he turn off these strong feelings? Why couldn't he have worked with the relationship they'd had and seen where things were going wrong? He wanted to fix things, but what if he was too late? What if he'd lost it all forever and once that stamp of failure had been placed on their union, there would be no resolving the situation?

The intimacy, the passion…his wife had been everything. But she thought she was making the right move for both of them—so why were they both utterly shattered now?

"Now who's the one thinking?" she asked, tipping her head and raising her brows.

Her hands came up to the little tie right between the swell of her breasts as she gave a tug, her eyes never wavering from his. Camden couldn't look away, but he sure as hell could help speed up this process. He made quick work of shedding his own clothes and a moment later, the corset peeled back and fell to the floor behind her, leaving her entire body completely bare and beautifully exposed.

"You're still so damn perfect."

He reached for her once again, lifting her up with his hands on her round backside until she wrapped her legs around his waist. Camden crossed the room to the bed and pressed her back against the thick post.

Her hands were all over him, her core hovering just above where he still ached for her. She'd always done that to him. He'd never been able to deny her anything…at least in the bedroom.

"Slow down," he whispered against her shoulder as he trailed his lips over her heated skin. "No need to rush when we have all night."

She trembled again.

No, that wasn't a tremble. That was a cringe. She'd flat-out recoiled against him and in that instant, Camden had the realization that they had very different plans for the night…much like their different views for their marriage.

Slowly, he eased her back down and took a step away. How could he have made such a mistake? To think he could slide right back into her life like they didn't have a mound of problems driving a wedge between them.

Raking his hand through his hair, Cam turned and headed across the room toward his clothes. There was nothing left here for him, for them. He could want the hell out of her, he could have her many times over, but that wouldn't change the fact she had already checked out. He'd hoped, even put a little faith in thinking they would be intimate after months apart and she'd see just how good they were together. That she would be reminded of when and how they fell in love to begin with.

As Camden dressed, Delilah said nothing. He couldn't help but risk a glance her way. She stood there, hands at her sides, completely bare. Her hair was still tossed about her shoulders, her lips swollen, her eyes now filled with unshed tears.

This entire scene summed up their lives. Hot and passionate fighting against angst and brokenness.

His heart ached, but at the same time, he couldn't back down on how much he wanted this marriage to work and apparently she couldn't forgo the idea that they weren't meant to be. And maybe they were simply two different people who hadn't gotten beyond the heat before they said "I do," but he didn't think so. If there wasn't something tangible between them, then this split wouldn't hurt so damn bad.

"I can't do all night." She blinked and glanced away, wrapping her arms around her midsection. "Not anymore. It's just… I can't."

He'd pushed too far. He'd wanted to spend hours

with his wife, wake up to her lying against him and make love to her all over again. She wanted fast, frantic sex in the front seat of a car, and to sleep alone.

Who the hell had he become? He'd never been a man like this. Before he met Dee, Camden had been all about the flings and the one-night stands. Now he balked at the idea of anything temporary. He'd seen too much damage between couples in his line of work and had vowed never to marry, but then Delilah came into his life and nothing had been the same.

Who the hell had a one-night stand with their spouse?

Soon-to-be ex.

He still wasn't ready to let that thought turn into a reality and he wasn't going to let her give up. He could fight hard enough for both of them because Delilah never just quit on anything…except him.

Camden had nothing to say. What else could there be? She wanted one thing, he wanted another, nobody was compromising, but they both wanted sex. Their relationship was as simple and complex as that.

"Things didn't have to be this way," she told him, turning her focus away.

Cam pulled in a deep breath and sighed, still unsure what he could say to defend himself that hadn't already been put out there.

"No, they didn't," he agreed. "I only wanted—"

"I know what you wanted, but that just isn't possible."

Her voice cracked and so did his heart. This wasn't going to go anywhere productive tonight. Their emotions were too raw and coming off of sex certainly wasn't the time to figure anything out. Not only that, she was still recovering from Milly's death. He should have known her heart was too vulnerable, too exposed to handle anything else.

Despite everything happening around her and to her, Delilah would never admit vulnerability. But there was only so much someone could take and he wanted to make sure he was there for her when she broke. He would never walk away from the one good and solid person in his life.

Maybe his actions made him selfish or a masochist, he didn't know. But he did know he had to take things day by day and maybe even hour by hour.

Silence settled heavy between them, driving the wedge deeper. Camden didn't want to wait any longer. He had to get out of here. She needed her space right now and, quite honestly, so did he.

He turned, letting himself out the way he'd come in. Getting his wife back had been his main goal since she moved out, but after tonight, he didn't even know if that was possible anymore and he came to the damning realization that this might end in defeat.

Three

"Why are we in the boardroom?"

Sara and Elise both glanced up from the obscenely long table as Delilah stood in the doorway with her bag and phone in one hand and her Angel's Share insulated coffee mug in the other. There was not enough caffeine for this day. Not only had she overslept and forgotten all about the meeting *she* had scheduled, she'd barely gotten any sleep last night after Camden had left.

Her body still hummed from the all-too-brief encounter, but they'd still managed to screw up the night. Or rather, she had. But she was done holding in her thoughts for fear of hurt feelings. They were both already hurt and they deserved honesty on every level. Not clearing things up was how they'd gotten into this mess to begin with. She'd gone along with everything believing a picture-perfect life could be theirs simply because love and physical attraction should have been enough, right? She'd believed everything would work itself out.

Another life lesson learned the hard way.

"We're in the boardroom because we're having a meeting," Sara stated, then glanced at her watch. "That started twenty minutes ago."

"I had a bad morning."

That was the only excuse Delilah was ready to give right now. Between the soon-to-be ex who'd blown her mind in the front seat of his car last night and the fact she and her sisters had just had their lives torn upside down and inside out with the loss of their beloved Milly, it was a miracle there was only coffee in her mug this morning.

"You look like hell."

Delilah pulled out a chair and glanced at Elise. "You look lovely today, too. Thank you."

"You know what I mean," Elise amended with an eye roll. "Stay out too late dancing the night away at the charity event?"

Taking a sip of her coffee seemed like the logical step here in lieu of answering. She set her mug back down and dug into her bag for the folder she'd grabbed off her desk before coming into the boardroom.

"So I know we all have mentioned moving Angel's Share into a venue for weddings and other events," she started, still dodging any question regarding last night. "Well, I was contacted by the governor's wife and they want to have their daughter's wedding here next year. So, that does give us some time to hone in on costs and setup options. Then there's the drink side we need to consider—"

"Hold up."

Delilah stopped as Sara held up her hand.

"Can we get back to why you were late and why you look like you haven't slept in days?" her sister asked. "Because this definitely isn't like our usual Delilah. After that, we'll get to the topic of weddings because Elise and Antonio will be wed on this property first."

Delilah glanced from Sara to Elise and noted both ladies were staring at her fixedly. Clearly they were not going any further until she answered some questions. She should have known they'd see right through her and that she'd not get away with dodging them so easily. Had the roles been reversed, she'd also demand to know what was up.

Unfortunately, Delilah didn't have the answers. Oh, she certainly had the facts of everything that happened, but anything beyond that was a hard no. The why and the how were still muddled in her mind and she didn't know if she'd ever fully comprehend the unbreakable bond to Cam. Would she ever be able to make a break from the one relationship that was toxic?

"I know you were worried about running into Cam's parents," Sara added. "Is that what happened?"

That might have been less dramatic and heartbreaking than the way things ultimately ended. At least she could have walked away from them. There was no ignoring that invisible pull toward her husband.

"They weren't there and the charity event was fine," Delilah admitted. "I didn't actually stay too long, but I did get the Angel's Share donation in."

She might have forgotten last night and only done so this morning via a few clicks on her computer, but she still managed to get it in, which was all that mattered. She had left too early and missed the silent auction, so she added a little extra to her online support.

"Please tell me you didn't go as that ridiculous shadow idea," Elise groaned.

"I'll have you know that costume was a brilliant idea for someone who wanted to go unnoticed," she defended with a slight lift of her chin.

"Hard to go unnoticed when the hostess was trying to fix you up with someone," Sara murmured with a snicker. "Did you actually see this guy?"

Saw him, danced with him, had sex in the front seat of his car.

"It was Camden."

The gasp from both sisters echoed in the boardroom. But, in true Sara fashion, her shock turned to delight.

"That's wonderful," she squealed with a clasp of her hands. "You two are meant to be. You'll realize it yourself. I just hope it's before you guys sign those papers."

Sara always had hearts dancing around her head. The woman believed in all the fairy tales they'd watched as children. And true love had worked out and triumphed for Elise and Antonio, but things just weren't meant to be for Delilah.

This conversation would lead to absolutely nowhere. Delilah had explained to both of her sisters when the marriage started falling apart that just because there's chemistry doesn't mean there's a solid foundation. And just because she wanted and wished—none of that could make miracles happen.

"Sara, you are going to have to get this reunion out of your head. Cam and I are getting divorced. There's too much between us that only we know, but trust me. It's over."

Sara's eyes widened and her lips thinned. Delilah didn't mean to be rude, but she also couldn't let her sisters believe any untruth. Keeping that sliver of hope among her small circle would only cause more heartache down the road.

"The modified papers should be in anytime," Delilah went on. "And once they're signed, I can move on."

Silence settled in the spacious room as her sisters continued to stare at her with concerned expressions. No matter what they thought about her situation, Delilah was ultimately the one who would have to live with these decisions.

"Do you want to talk about the root of the problem?" Elise asked after a moment. "I mean, we've tried to give you your space, but it's been months and we've all been through so much since then. We simply want to help."

Delilah nodded, knowing her sisters only wanted what was best for her. But no matter how much they were there for each other, there wasn't a thing they could do to fix this mess.

"I don't want any of this to bring down the high that Angel's Share is on or your engagement," she told Elise. "Let me handle things my way and you all go on about your lives."

Elise rolled her eyes. "You honestly think we're just going to ignore the issue simply because it's tough? And you aren't bringing anything down. This is life. It can be chaotic, sad, happy, a mess—you just never know. We're here for all of it."

Delilah pulled in a shaky breath and really tried

not to bust out into the emotional breakdown she was barely holding back.

"Can we just shift our focus to your wedding so I can get back to the governor about his daughter?" Delilah asked, hoping they went with her lead.

When both sisters nodded, so much weight lifted from Delilah's shoulders. Finally, she could focus on something she could control...work. This was where she could shine, where she had the most confidence and could really be herself.

Since the gala, overseeing new VIP clients was now her territory instead of Elise's, who was bogged down in sales. But as they ventured into becoming a rental venue for parties and weddings, Dee was champing at the bit to really spread her wings, adding Event Coordinator to her résumé. The more work, the better.

"Have you all set a date?" Delilah asked.

Elise nodded. "Finally. We're looking at something soon and small. I wanted spring, but that weather is so unpredictable and I'm in a hurry to marry the man of my dreams."

Delilah forced her smile in place, trying to be happy for her sister and not compare the two relationships. Elise and Antonio were absolutely perfect for each other. They'd met when he'd come from Spain to do a tour of vineyards and distilleries in the States and they'd immediately fallen in love.

No way would Delilah let her own personal life put some dark cloud over her sister's happily-ever-after. Because no matter how her own marriage had started and ended, Delilah did believe love was for some people. Elise and Antonio were living proof.

"Any other details you want to share?" Sara asked. "Colors, dress ideas, food."

Elise pursed her lips and shrugged. "I was thinking I should probably hire a wedding planner, but I don't know if anyone is even available for something so soon with barely any notice. Most brides take over a year to plan these things."

"A wedding planner?" Sara gasped. "Why would you do that when you have two sisters?"

Elise glanced from Sara to Delilah. "You two want to help? I just assumed we were all too busy to take on something like this."

"A wedding?" Sara laughed. "I've been preparing for this my entire life."

Sara tapped on her computer, then on the control panel in the middle of the table, and within moments, a spreadsheet popped up on the drop screen behind Elise's head. Sara reached across the table once more to dim the lights.

"The plan really should go in this exact order for a flawless, magical day," Sara began.

Delilah stared, completely stunned at this extremely detailed list. Though she shouldn't be surprised. Of the three sisters with their vastly different personalities, Sara had always been the hopeless romantic and she was just waiting for her knight to ride into town.

Delilah, on the other hand, wasn't waiting for anyone to save her or make her future complete. She was making her own way and didn't want someone else slaying her proverbial dragons.

"I'm not sure I need quite this much of a presentation," Elise told her sister. "It's all a bit overwhelming and we aren't wanting anything so grand."

Sara's brows drew in; her lips turned into a slight frown. "Nothing grand? Are you going to elope all alone with just a plain old dress and no flowers, too?"

Elise's eyes darted to Delilah.

"Oh, sorry," Sara murmured. "I didn't think."

Delilah smacked her hands on the glossy tabletop, causing both sisters to jump.

"Stop tiptoeing around me," she exclaimed. "Yes, I eloped. No, I didn't have flowers, but my dress was new. Yes, I'm getting divorced. And, yes, I slept with Cam last night—"

"What?"

"Well, damn."

Elise and Sara both spoke at the same time and Dee realized she'd let her secret slip. She sank back in her chair and let out a deep breath as she tried to collect her thoughts and figure out a way to backpedal.

But the words were already out and there was no taking them back.

Delilah closed her eyes. "Can we pretend I didn't say that?"

"Not likely," Elise replied. "But if you don't want to talk about it, we can table that discussion for now."

Well, that was something because she wasn't ready to face her feelings on the night, let alone talk about it and be asked questions she had no answers for.

She risked looking back at her sisters and instead of seeing judgment, all she saw was compassion. She'd almost prefer the judgment. Knowing they felt sorry for her really grated on her last nerve, but she knew they cared. They weren't the enemy and she had no reason to put her frustration on them. She had nobody to blame but herself… and Cam. It took two to make or break a marriage.

"Let's recap." Elise ticked off on her fingers. "We have a high-society wedding to plan, after my big day of course, and we need to get started on that with a calmer checklist than what Sara has, Dee slept with Cam even though they're divorcing, and we're going to only discuss business until Delilah says otherwise. Did that sum up our meeting?"

Dee knew Elise was only trying to make light

of everything, so she couldn't help but add her own bit.

"Should we go ahead and throw in searching for our biological fathers or is that too much for a morning meeting?"

"That's definitely too much," Sara agreed, nodding her head. "I mean, we do need to talk about what all is going on now that we know the truth, or part of it anyway."

Losing Milly and finding out they all three had different fathers on top of everything else going on was enough to have them leaning on each other a little more than usual.

"Listen," Delilah started. "I know that I'm cranky, I know I look like hell this morning—"

"Sorry about that," Elise chimed in.

"No worries. It's the truth. I'm just in a pretty bumpy spot in my life, but I'll get back on track."

Her cell buzzed on the table and she glanced at the screen. Her heart immediately leaped up into her throat.

I don't regret last night

When her eyes focused back on Sara, her sister smiled. "Are you ready to talk yet?"

Delilah wanted to, but not here and not when they had so much else to do. Angel's Share was such a big part of their lives and required one hundred percent from each of them if they were going to continue to grow and dominate this industry. They didn't come this far to start slowing down or get too relaxed.

She wanted nothing more than to confide in her sisters because they would support her and offer sound advice. But she just wasn't ready. Her head was too cloudy to try to process anything they'd say and she had a terrible feeling once she started talking, she'd start breaking down, and she'd never been a pretty crier.

Her eyes slid over her screen once more and those nerves in her belly swirled again at Camden's words.

Because, if she was being honest with herself, she didn't regret last night, either.

Four

Delilah had just pulled some leftover takeout from the microwave when her cell rang. She sat the unopened box on the kitchen island and tapped her cell, putting the call on speaker.

"Hello."

"Dee, it's Alisha. Is this a bad time?"

"No, of course not. How can I help you?"

"I'm so sorry to bother you after hours, but I had to call and apologize."

Delilah eased the box open and eyed the two-day-old fried rice. She really needed to hit the grocery store.

"Why are you apologizing?" Delilah asked. "I had to slip out early, so if anyone is apologizing, it should be me."

"Oh, I was so busy I didn't know when you left," she admitted. "But, I just found out that Camden is your husband. Well, almost ex. I'm mortified I was trying to set you guys up."

Yeah, well, it worked. Moments after the meetup, they were having sex in his car.

"Don't be sorry or embarrassed," Delilah soothed. "You had no idea and I appreciate the gesture that you were trying to make my evening a little nicer, so thank you."

Alisha laughed. "Well, I didn't expect a thanks, but I'll take it. I felt so bad when my brother told me. I honestly had no idea and we're both still new to the area, so I'm finding my footing. Your donation was extremely generous and so appreciated, by the way."

"My sisters and I are happy to support our community and worthy causes. From what I saw, you had a rather successful night."

"We did. The children will certainly benefit from all the kindness poured out from this community."

Another call popped up on her screen and Delilah recognized the name of the real estate agent she'd used to secure this rental.

"Alisha, I'm sorry, but I have to take this other call," Dee told her.

"Oh, no worries. Thanks again and I'm still sorry for my mistake."

"You're welcome and I'll text you about lunch. I still need to hear about that engagement."

"I can't wait."

Dee tapped her screen and answered the other call.

"Hey, Kayla."

"Delilah. Is this a good time?"

She stared at the less than appealing leftovers and finally closed the box and put it back in the fridge. Now that she was alone, cooking for one just seemed a waste of her energy.

"Perfect time," Delilah replied. "Is everything okay?"

"As a matter of fact, yes," Kayla told her. "I have a proposition that came my way and I need to pass it along to you. Now, don't immediately give me your answer. This is something you'll need to think about."

Delilah stood in front of her fridge, staring at the bag of bagels and the carton of eggs, wondering if either were in date. When was the last time she'd even gone to the grocery? She wondered how quick something could be delivered.

"What is it?" Dee asked.

"I have a client who is moving to the Benton Springs area in the next month and she wants to buy your house."

Delilah spun around and eyed her cell on the counter. "My house? As in, the one I'm renting?"

"Um…no. As in the one you and Camden still own together."

Delilah gripped the edge of the countertop and pulled in a deep breath. Someone wanted her house? No, it wasn't hers. Well, legally she was part owner, but she wouldn't be going back and she didn't know how Cam would feel about selling. She actually assumed he'd stay there while she found her footing elsewhere.

That was one of the modifications needed in their divorce papers. She'd wanted the house put back in his name since he'd bought the place before they were married. There was no need for her to have any part of his past since she wouldn't be part of his future.

Yet, she'd loved that house. When Cam had first shown her his place, she'd fallen in love with the views down into the valley. Living up on a hill and being secluded had been absolutely perfect for them.

As memories started to hit her hard, the lump of regret and sadness threatened to overtake her. She had to stay positive, she had to keep looking to her future, because if she fell back into life with Camden, she knew in the end she'd be a letdown to not only him, but his family. Something he would never admit, but she wasn't stupid or naive and she didn't want to be the driving force that eventually tore him and his parents apart.

"I honestly have no clue about selling," Delilah finally answered. "I can talk to Camden and let you know or have him call you directly since the home will legally be his soon."

"That would be great. I'm definitely not pressuring either of you, but the opportunity is here now if you think selling is a possibility. I promised my client I would present their offer."

Delilah nodded, though no one could see her. Words were becoming difficult to get past that growing lump in her throat. If he sold, that would be another portion of their life together that was lost forever.

"Try to get back to me when you can," Kayla went on. "I'll be showing my client other properties as well, but I just remembered your home checked off all their boxes."

Yeah, that home had checked off all of her and Cam's boxes, too. They'd christened every room, and as much as she'd loved their physical relationship, she'd also craved the simple things that never happened. Sitting on the front porch swing with a glass of wine at the end of the day or enjoying the hot tub on the back deck while under the stars. But he traveled so much, meeting with his elite clients, and she had been busy here working on the distillery.

Delilah ended the call and sent a text to Cam.

Her hands shook, which was absurd. This was part of the moving-on process she wanted…she *needed*.

We have to talk

She gripped her cell as she headed down the hallway toward her bedroom. Dinner was the farthest thing from her mind. Suddenly all she wanted to do was curl into a ball and cry at the thought of their home going to someone else. Yes, she'd left, but that had been because she couldn't handle staying and living with all of those memories. But, selling, if that's what Cam was interested in, would be another final step of closure in this new journey.

She knew she couldn't have her life both ways. She was either in or out and she'd chosen to leave. There was too much between them and ultimately, she knew if she stayed, Cam would end up resenting her and she'd start wondering if she'd ever come ahead of his job.

A nice bath and a glass of wine was what she needed. She'd been trying to focus on self-care lately when time allowed and if there was ever a day she needed to unwind, it was today. Everything seemed to be closing in all around her and she just wanted to take a step back from reality.

While she loved her work, she threw herself even harder into it when she and Cam first split.

Her sisters finally made her realize that working to exhaustion wasn't the way to deal with a broken heart. The distraction might work for a short time, but ultimately did more harm than good.

Delilah checked her cell as she placed it on her bathroom vanity. No reply from Cam. She shouldn't be surprised. That part had always been an issue. Communication...or lack thereof. He'd been married to his job before they came together, but she thought she might actually get bumped up in the ranks of his priority list.

Clearly that never happened.

She drew her bath, poured in a generous dose of her favorite lavender bubble bath and headed back to the kitchen for the wine. No doubt when she and Cam finally talked, he would want to discuss the other night, but she had to bank that experience as another memory. Never again would she be intimate with her soon-to-be ex. Their time was over and she was officially moving on—broken heart and all.

The entire day had been one headache after another. Demanding clients seeking the impossible and refusing to budge only left him with more frustration than usual. Of course, it could also be his own personal life spiraling out of control that contributed to his migraines as of late. But he'd already had to plan yet another trip to Texas to meet with one client who really should star in her own *Housewives* show. Nothing was ever good enough and if she laid out one more demand, Camden wasn't above dropping her or giving her an ultimatum.

He'd stayed at the office much too long, longer than usual. The sun had set hours ago and he headed through the dark, winding roads that led to his home on top of a hill on the edge of town. He'd been working himself too hard, not taking breaks, throwing himself into everything his clients needed or wanted, and booking extra trips. Anything to exorcise Delilah from his mind...but clearly nothing was working.

What he needed was a damn break.

No. What he needed was his wife back.

Delilah had called and texted a few times and he hadn't gotten a chance to call her. Each time he picked up his phone to contact her, something else would pop up that needed his immediate attention. Then his father had called and that conversation had been the proverbial cherry on top.

Camden's lights slashed through the darkness, landing on the two-story home he'd shared with Delilah for five years. The place had been so perfect for them, but with her gone, it seemed so damn empty and depressing. He'd never noticed when he'd lived here alone before they got together, but now, the void was all too obvious.

He tried to only come home to sleep and shower.

Other than that, he kept himself busy and out of the home that held way too much history.

As he approached, Camden recognized the black car in the drive and his gut tightened. He didn't know whether to be excited or worried. The woman had his emotions all over the place these last several months.

Delilah parked in her old spot just in front of her garage door where she had for all the years they'd been married. That sight shoved him right back to all the times he took for granted she'd always be there.

Camden pulled up beside her, confused that she'd shown up without warning, but she had called so maybe that's what she was trying to tell him. Definitely something she could have just texted, so something else must be going on.

Delilah did still have a few boxes in one of the spare bedrooms, but other than that, she'd cleared out most everything she wanted. That was something he wasn't going to fight over. He couldn't care less about a sofa or dishes. He could buy anything he wanted, including another house. He just wanted Delilah. Couldn't she see that? Didn't she understand that this giving up wasn't what either of them stood for? They were both fighters. They wouldn't have made it this far being so successful in their careers if they were passive people.

They also wouldn't have made it in five years of

marriage if they just threw in the proverbial towel when things got tough.

A quick glance told Camden that his wife wasn't in her car, but then he spotted her on the front porch in the swing. He was so damn tired and had planned on coming home, showering and crawling into bed. A new burst of energy suddenly spiraled through him at the opportunity that presented itself.

While he didn't know what brought her here, they needed to discuss how they'd left things. The last thing they needed was another issue coming between them…and he wouldn't mind another round of the other night.

Camden headed up the curved stone path leading to the steps. Delilah glanced up from her phone as he ascended to the porch. Her eyes immediately went to his, drawing him in. She pointed her bare toes on the concrete porch and stopped the swing. Without a word, he closed the distance and took a seat beside her. Once he was settled, she set the swing back into motion.

Moments ticked by in silence, with only the occasional squeak from the hinges of the swing.

"I always wanted this," she said after several minutes. "A starry evening, you on this swing with me as we discussed our day, maybe a glass of wine in hand. Not a care in the world. Impossible, I know, but it was a dream I had."

This was the first time they'd sat together on

this swing…ever. They'd been out back on their patio a couple of times, but never right in this spot. He'd had no clue this was something she'd always wanted. Had he ever asked? Or worse, had she told him and he didn't pay attention?

Why was she letting him inside her thoughts now? Did she want to drive that wedge deeper or make him feel like a complete jerk? Or maybe she just needed him to know before she walked away for good.

Maybe had he been more attentive to her and less to his job, they would have shared nights like she wanted. Camden had worked his ass off to get where he was. Then when they married, he worked just as diligently to keep her happy. He wanted to be her provider and assumed that was his role when they married. But Delilah needed no one to care for her. She could do anything on her own, and maybe that hurt his pride and ego a bit, but it was also another reason he'd fallen deeper for her. She was such an amazing woman, one that he'd been damn lucky to have.

But he hadn't let her go quite yet. They were still married, which meant there was still a chance to pull this marriage back to life.

"I can go get that glass of wine," he offered.

"It's a little late."

She didn't mean the time of night and they both knew it. Delilah kept the swing moving gently and he wished like hell he could rewind time and sit just like she'd described.

"Sorry I didn't get back to you earlier," he told her. "I got so busy and… I know that's not a good excuse, but it's the truth."

She remained silent as the swing kept moving. He waited for her to reply or tell him that was the problem with their marriage, but what came out of her mouth was certainly unexpected.

"Kayla called and has a buyer for this house."

Cam planted his feet flat and stopped the swaying swing. His focus immediately went to Dee, who was staring straight ahead as if she hadn't just dropped a monumental statement between them that would continue to take them further apart.

"Are we selling this house?" he asked, shocked she'd even mention such a thing.

She shrugged, but still didn't look his way. What was she thinking? Is this why she had come? Did she want him to get rid of this aspect of their lives together?

"What did you tell Kayla?"

Now Delilah shifted her attention to him, lifting her knee between them and stretching her arm along the back of the swing. She blew out a sigh and seemed as frustrated and lost as he was…all the confirmation he needed to see that she was having doubts or at least she wasn't happy with their current arrangement.

"I told her I'd have to talk to you and that in the end the house would go back to your name and you'd have the final say."

Camden could hardly tolerate sitting here talking about the end of everything like this was the new normal. Which it was, but still. This wasn't right and neither of them were happy, so why the hell was he letting this go on?

They both had been through so much, at the expense of their pride, their happiness—his parents' behavior, the death of Milly. Everything had come crashing down around them and they were buried beneath the rubble.

Something had to change because this entire situation couldn't keep going on. He needed a break and he wanted time with Delilah without all this outside noise around them. They had so much negativity knocking them from all sides.

Was it any wonder they'd fallen apart? Other than their honeymoon, they hadn't done anything for just themselves or to help this marriage be successful. Oh, she'd accompanied him a few times on a business trip here and there, but that wasn't the same. That was still work and one of the main issues she had with him.

"Come away with me."

Delilah's eyes widened as she jerked back at his

demand. He was a little shocked that his thoughts had been spoken aloud, too, but he wasn't sorry. Now he had to hurry and justify his outburst so he didn't look like a selfish bastard who just wanted to carry on what they'd been doing the other night. There was more to their relationship than sex… there had to be.

"We need this, Dee," he told her. "I know we're separated—"

"We filed for divorce. Twice, actually, since the first papers were wrong."

"But we still want each other," he retorted. "Just come away with me for a long weekend. Our work can wait. Hell, everything can wait."

Delilah rubbed her forehead and laughed. "You're not making any sense. We can't just run away, Cam. We're not going to be married as soon as we sign those papers. And even if we went away for a few days, everything will be waiting on us when we get back."

"Name the last time we put us first," he demanded. "Never. We never have. Just give me the next four days away from this place to show you that this marriage isn't a loss. We don't have to call it quits because things are hard. After four days, if you still want to sign those papers, I won't fight against it."

Though he had zero intention of losing this final battle because watching her walk away one last time would destroy him. He never wanted to face a reality where losing was part of his story. And he didn't want to face a reality without Delilah.

Just because she moved out and they filed those damn papers didn't mean he could turn off his feelings so quickly or as easily. All he wanted was one more chance to prove to her that they could build on what they started, and there had to be some way they could come to terms.

They needed to get back to the basics they'd skipped years ago. Maybe then she would see how serious he was about her and their future and about making this marriage the most successful part of both of their lives.

"I'm asking for four days." He stopped resisting and finally placed a hand on her thigh. "If you're afraid to be alone with me, then that should tell you that we still have reason to be together. That pull hasn't gone away, Dee. And if you go and feel nothing, then we'll go our separate ways."

But he knew that would be impossible. The way they combusted in the front seat of his car the other night was all the proof he needed that they had so much more time together. He couldn't just erase that hope.

"You expect me to believe you're going to put your work on hold for four days?" she asked with a disbelieving snicker.

He needed her to see just how serious he was

and that he wasn't playing games. If that meant putting his entire life on hold for a while, then so be it.

"You can hold on to my phone for those days." Camden held her gaze, making sure she knew just how invested he truly was. "I won't work even one minute."

She blinked as if she couldn't believe what he was saying. The quiet night surrounded them and the fact that she hadn't flat out said no really spoke volumes. He couldn't give her the chance to turn him down. This getaway might be exactly what they both needed…what they should have done at the first sign of trouble.

But that was the problem with broken hearts and couples splitting. He'd seen it all for years. Everything was a slow progression. People didn't decide to split up in the blink of an eye. Something seemingly harmless would wedge its way into a couple's life and that wedge would only expand because it had gone unnoticed.

Never in his life did he think this would happen to Delilah and him. Of course he was used to seeing marriages fall apart, but he never would have put himself in that same bracket. Maybe that was just his pride, but right now, Camden didn't feel as if he had much left to cling to.

In his vast experience and the high-society clientele he'd worked with, there was usually a healthy level of greed associated with the divorce.

One partner found someone they felt was better or they wanted money and freedom. There was always something they were moving on to and they always thought it was better than what they already had.

But that wasn't the case with Delilah and him. They had no one else and he never wanted anyone else. She was it for him and he'd damn well prove that to her until she understood how much she mattered.

"What about your parents?" she whispered.

"I'm not inviting them."

A hint of a smile danced over her lips, which was exactly what he wanted. He needed to see her genuinely smile, to know he put that emotion back in her. He didn't want her to associate only her negative or sad feelings with him. There was once a time when she was either laughing or loving. He hadn't seen those emotions from her in far too long.

Damn it. How had he let this aspect of his life become so faded into the background? Anything worth having and worth succeeding at should be first and foremost.

"You know what I mean," she corrected, the grin gone.

Camden nodded. "There's no reason they need to know what we're doing in our lives."

"But they do. They always know and they never wanted this marriage from the start."

Cam squeezed her leg. "I didn't grow up waiting to be married to who my parents approved of. I wanted to marry you, so I did."

There was too much history to get into tonight and all he wanted was a confirmed yes for this trip. But if he gave her too much time, she'd back out and let her fears and doubts cloud her judgment.

"Say yes and I'll have the pilot ready tomorrow morning," he told her. "Just… Damn it, Dee. Give in to what you want."

She closed her eyes and tipped her head back. He knew the thoughts that were swirling around in her head. The pros and cons were slamming together and Camden wasn't going to give her an opportunity to turn him down. He wanted time alone with his wife, the woman he still couldn't get enough of after five years of marriage.

"Stop trying to rationalize everything," he ordered. "Go with what you want, not with what you think is right."

She pulled in a deep breath and faced him once again. "I just don't want to prolong this pain."

Damn it. He understood exactly what she meant, but what if this ended in something far better than either of them intended? If there was even an inkling of a chance, he was going to wade through this mess they'd created and grab hold of that sliver of hope.

"We've already said we're ending the marriage," he told her. "So if you need to think of this as one last fling, that's fine. But I'm taking this trip as an attempt to show you that we shouldn't give up when there is still something there worth fighting for."

Her unshed tears glistened in the soft glow of the porch lights. Knowing he'd caused any amount of hurt was hands down the absolute worst part of this entire ordeal. All he'd wanted to do was be her support and her rock, financially and emotionally, yet somehow in his warped way of thinking, he'd screwed everything up.

Camden came to his feet and stared down at her. "I'll be at the airport at ten in the morning. That will give us both time to let anyone know that we are unavailable for the next few days. My plane will be ready and all you have to do is show up with a packed suitcase. Destination is a surprise if you decide to come."

Delilah stood as well and chewed on her bottom lip, a sure sign she was thinking this proposal through.

He waited for her to reply, but she merely stepped around him and off the porch. Cam turned and watched as she got into her car and drove away into the night. He stood there for quite a while after those taillights disappeared, wondering if he'd see her tomorrow, but also wondering if he'd pushed her too far.

Five

"This is the most ridiculous thing I've ever done," Delilah muttered to herself as she turned into the airport lot for the private planes.

One last time. This would be the last thing she did as a married woman with her husband. A getaway was exactly what she'd wanted while they'd been married and she deserved this, damn it. Not only had she thrust herself even deeper into her work since the split, she couldn't deny that the idea of having him alone for a few days had stirred her desires all over again.

So what if she was only thinking of herself right now? When she and Camden weren't discussing heavy topics or having guilt trips laid on them, they enjoyed each other's company…both in bed and out. She'd take these final four days and be completely and utterly selfish.

After all, she was sacrificing her own happiness so that he could find his.

In the long run, he would thank her. He wouldn't want to live in the middle of her and his family forever. That wasn't fair to any of them and sure as hell not the way a marriage should go.

Delilah pulled into the spot closest to his private hangar and cursed herself again for being so damn easy. He'd dangled sex and a mystery trip in front of her and she'd just packed so fast and sent out texts to her sisters, ready to go last night.

So what? She was human and she had needs. A trip with a man she knew could make her wildest fantasies come true...what woman would turn that down? Besides, he'd already given her the out she wanted. At the end of the four days, he wouldn't argue anymore about signing those papers. This trip was a win-win all the way around.

After messaging her sisters last night, they'd both been understandably nosy and concerned. Delilah only told them she was taking a few days off and getting out of town. She didn't tell them with whom because she had been too tired for the phone calls or late-night visits that would have very likely ensued.

As Delilah pulled her suitcase from her trunk, Camden stepped up beside her.

"You're late."

She couldn't help but bite back a grin. "Only ten minutes."

When she turned to face him, she noted he wasn't smiling as he lifted her luggage from the car. His brows were drawn in and he'd obviously been legitimately worried she wouldn't show.

Interesting. Maybe he wasn't only in this for the physical getaway, but that's exactly how she had to go into these next few days. Her heart had no place here…she wouldn't be that naive again. If she opened up that wound once more, she feared she may never heal and properly move on.

He sat the suitcase down and reached into his pocket.

"As promised."

Camden handed over his cell and she was positively stunned. The man lived on that device, but he wasn't one to scroll on social media. He was all work, all the time. The lifeline between his clients and him was always open, no matter the time of day or night. Owning his own firm meant more responsibility. He took so much pride in being the best in his field and making a name for himself.

Which is just one way they complemented each other so well. They'd been drawn by that work ethic at first.

No, actually they'd been drawn in by lust, but

the get-to-know-you phase came later and they quickly realized how much they had in common.

Delilah took the phone and slid it into her purse. "I can't believe you are relinquishing this for the entire trip."

Cam released the luggage handle and closed the distance between them. Before she realized his intentions, he had her face framed between his strong hands, but with a delicate touch as he stared into her eyes.

"There are more important things right now and the only thing I'm doing on this trip is my wife."

Desire curled low in her belly and she wondered if they'd even make it to their destination before they tore each other's clothes off. Their encounter the other night had only reminded her of how amazing they were together—physically, anyway. And every moment since then, she'd wanted him all over again.

But something even more concerning than desire hit her. Delilah's heart flipped. Damn it. Hadn't she just told herself her heart couldn't get involved? She'd very carefully removed herself from his world and tried to delicately unweave each thread of their former life together.

She'd wanted to come before his career for the past five years, but it seemed he always just assumed she'd be around. There were times he'd figured if he bought her a piece of jewelry or had a designer come to the house to create any new seasonal pieces she wanted, that would make up for the void in his absence. Being bribed with materialistic things wasn't how she was raised and that wasn't the marriage she wanted.

Although, he'd just said she was important for right now, so maybe he was fine temporarily putting work aside. Long term, though…that was another story. The five years they'd been married had been truly a feat and she was shocked they'd made it that far.

"Where are we going?" she asked.

His eyes dropped to her mouth, then back up to her eyes as he smiled. "It's a surprise."

When he released her and took a step back, Delilah pulled in a breath and willed her desires and bundle of nerves to relax. It wasn't like she hadn't been alone with her husband before.

But this is the last time.

Just the idea of something being final had that familiar lump of sorrow forming in her throat. Leaving had been the most difficult decision she'd made, but she'd gotten stuck in this rut of working and coming home to an empty house because Cam always stayed so late at the office. The cycle had to be broken and she was the one who had made the decision to step aside and make a better way.

This break would be good for them. They'd

come into this relationship hot for each other so it was only fitting they…what? Have an exit fling?

Good heavens. This sounded even more ridiculous than she'd first thought. Who went on a final romantic trip with their spouse? Most people getting a divorce were thrilled to be rid of them and threw divorce parties. Not Delilah. She'd packed lingerie for the occasion.

"There you go thinking again," he scolded. "I can see it. You get this look on your face like you're having some mental conversation trying to decide if what you're doing is right or wrong."

He knew her so well—of course he'd recognize her uncertainty. Even though she'd voiced her concerns for quite some time now, Cam knew her thoughts, but he'd never called her out before. Living with someone for five years would make you pretty in tune to their emotions. She just never thought he was paying that much attention… Perhaps he was. Or, at least he was now.

"This just feels…odd."

He took her hand like he had many times over the years and led her to his awaiting plane. The pilot stood at the base of the steps and nodded his greeting with a tip of his hat.

"I've seen it all when it comes to divorces," he assured her. "Taking a trip before ending things is about the least crazy thing I've heard."

She recalled a few of the outlandish stories he'd

tell her about some of the firm's clients. Of course he never told names for privacy reasons, but a few of the divorce stories were enough to make her feel better about herself and this trip she'd agreed to. At least she hadn't asked for an exorbitant clothing and shoe allowance on top of alimony like one of his clients.

"I hope I packed the right things," she said as he handed over the luggage to the pilot.

Cam gestured for her to go ahead of him onto the steps. "You didn't have to pack anything as far as I'm concerned."

Delilah rolled her eyes. "Of course you'd say that. I actually packed a little of everything to cover all my bases since you didn't tell me where we were going."

She mounted the steps and ducked her head as she stepped into the aircraft. They hadn't used this plane much considering one or both were always too busy with work to take vacations. When she'd mention taking time off to spend together or to just get away from their hectic schedules, he would always say the timing wasn't right for him…ultimately, she finally just quit asking.

On two rare occasions, he took a trip to meet high-profile clients when she'd tagged along, but still every aspect was all about work. He had stayed busy with meetings and she'd found random things to do around the town. Lonely and boring—

two other adjectives she didn't want to describe her marriage. No relationship should be that way and she deserved better. So did Cam, which was why they shouldn't be together. If she left, maybe he'd realize that there was more and that he should want something beyond work and being the most sought-out lawyer in his field.

Delilah looked around trying to decide where to sit. No matter where, she assumed Cam would cozy next to her and very likely get this romantic trip underway. Nerves danced in her belly at the anticipation. She had to keep reminding herself these next few days were only part of their final goodbye...this wasn't the time to rekindle anything because the end result would be the same.

Delilah opted for a seat on the leather couch and sank into the buttery-soft material. The two sofas on either side of the aisle were much cozier than the plush chairs in the back. She crossed her legs and waited for Cam to board. She assumed he was talking to the pilot.

Moments later, Camden came on board and headed toward the back of the plane where the bedroom and the kitchen were located. In all the times she'd wanted to escape, part had been because they needed to, but part had been because she'd never had such luxuries growing up. Not that she ever needed all the bling and high-society living. She loved her humble childhood where the main component was Milly teaching them all the ways to be independent and strong. Those were the life lessons instilled in her and now she was making a life she could be proud of.

Being married to Cam had spoiled her, though. She loved being on a team with a determined, successful man. A man who worked just as hard as she did and had an ethic that matched her own. She'd always figured if she married someone who didn't have that drive that there would be an imbalance. Perhaps she should have married someone completely opposite.

She truly wished she had the answers, and she wished turning off feelings could be a simple process without all the mess of confusion and pain. She didn't want anyone hurt by her actions of making that final decision, but she also couldn't let this marriage drag on any longer. She deserved more. They both did.

Camden reappeared with a bottle of wine in one hand and a full glass in the other. He took a seat next to her and handed over the stemless glass.

"I know you like to finish the bottle once it's open," he joked.

Delilah shrugged. "Cork stoppers are for quitters."

She swirled the contents and gave an obligatory sniff. Light and fruity, her favorite. While she loved the rich, earthy notes of a bourbon, she occasionally wanted something lighter.

"It's from a new vineyard in Georgia," he told her. "I have a client whose family owns it and he sent me a box of each of their varieties."

"You must have really done right by him to get that many boxes of wine."

"I'm good at what I do."

Delilah took a sip of the wine as worry spiraled through her. She'd trusted his firm to file the papers in accordance with what they had discussed. She didn't think he'd screw her over and she truly believed he cared for her in his own way…just not the way she needed him to care or to love.

"How is it?" he asked.

"Delicious."

She licked her lips to savor the taste and realized her mistake the moment her focus shifted to him. Those expressive eyes remained fixated on her mouth and that familiar stirring of desire slid through her. She had to set some ground rules or at least figure some things out before they went any further on this impromptu getaway.

Delilah gripped her glass as the plane taxied down the runway. If this trip had happened seven months ago, she would have been in heaven. Knowing that he was putting forth more effort into their marriage before she walked out would have definitely been a turning point in the right direction. She didn't always like to relinquish control, but she wouldn't have minded being whisked away on a spontaneous surprise trip. Unfortunately, that never happened and part of her felt like he was in a panic trying to save something that had already failed.

"I need to know what your expectations are here," she told him.

Camden nodded and settled back, his instant lawyer mode seeming to take over right before her eyes. He relaxed against the couch and extended his arm along the back. His fingers started toying with the ends of her hair as she fastened her belt. Another familiar moment she couldn't escape. Everything was familiar, comfortable…except for the part where this relationship and romantic trip had an expiration date.

"I have no expectations," he informed her. "Whatever happens will be up to you. Of course I want my wife in my bed. I've made no secret about the fact I never wanted this marriage to end. I can admit I haven't been the best husband. I thought I was doing what you needed, but…"

The plane lifted just as Delilah's stomach knotted up. She took another sip of the wine and then set it in the cup holder on the table at her side before shifting in her seat.

"Talking about the actual marriage is probably not a good idea." She tucked her hair behind her ear and chose her words carefully. "This trip isn't a reunion, Cam. This is our final goodbye. We're putting a lid on this box that holds our memories and our time together."

He edged closer, so close she could feel the warmth of his breath and breathe in that signature clean, woodsy scent of his cologne. She'd bought him that cologne last Christmas. She'd been out shopping and immediately knew he would love the scent. Just another reminder of something that was coming to an end. No more shopping for her husband for a holiday or birthday or any other special occasion.

"I'm not pressuring you for anything, but I'm also not ready to say goodbye," he murmured. "And no more talk of endings or marriages or anything outside of this trip. I just want to get back to who we were years ago when we didn't care about anything else but each other."

Those broken pieces of her heart shattered just a little more. She often thought back to when they first met. She traveled down their journey in her mind, wondering where things had started going wrong. But she could see now that they were doomed from the start.

If he wanted to only focus on them, she could work with that. At least she knew how everything was going to end and she could take these final days and have her fill of Camden. She'd use these memories to last her because there would be no more made after this.

"No marriage talk," she agreed, then sighed and steered the conversation to something else. "So, when are you going to tell me where we're going?"

"You'll see when we get there."

"Okay, then can you at least tell me how far it is?"

He shrugged. "Not far."

Delilah rolled her eyes and groaned. "You are such a lawyer with those vague answers."

"And you are terrible at waiting to see what your surprises are because you want everything planned in a nice, orderly fashion that you have total control of."

She picked up her drink again and swirled the last bit around. She should be offended, but he was dead-on. She did like to plan things and wanted her life just the way she mapped it out…which was why this whole divorce nearly destroyed her. Closing such an important chapter of her life, one that was supposed to be the happiest, was certainly never one of her life goals.

"You know I hate surprises," she muttered against the rim of her glass.

Camden laughed. "You love surprises, you just hate when someone else is doing the planning and you don't know all the details."

True. She did pride herself on control and having everything planned out. Her sisters always teased her for all of her planners growing up, but look at her now. Part owner of the country's only distillery run by women. That's why she was in charge of all new client accounts, too. She could get everything set up in a nice, uniform manner to make sure there were no bumps in the road.

"I didn't like that time you surprised me with lilies," she joked.

"I had no clue you were allergic," Cam defended.

That had been the first and last time he'd ever gotten her flowers because he'd been terrified of sending her to the emergency room again. He had surprised her in other ways, though. He'd randomly bring home her favorite takeout or have some gift delivered to their house. Then there were the clothes. So many clothes from designers he'd pay to come to their house. Most women would love such things, but she could shop just fine on her own.

Everything had boiled down to monetary things, which she appreciated, but then she started just wanting simplicity and his time instead of a gift. He had never been willing to give where it actually counted. Sacrificing his time from work or sacrificing a portion of his family to put her in that place would have made all the difference. She wished he would have stood up for her against his family before things spiraled out of control.

She didn't want to be his number one all day, every day. She completely understood he had a family and a career before her, but he'd never attempted to mesh all of those things. Didn't he understand that marriage took a lot of work? Had he believed that once they married the hard part of winning her was over?

She circled back to the fact they weren't going to discuss the marriage, which meant if she wanted to enjoy her trip, she needed to not think about all the ways they'd failed. She still cared for him, still enjoyed her time with him. So that is what she'd focus on.

"Can you just tell me if we're leaving the country?" she asked.

Camden reached over and topped off her wineglass. "We're staying in the US."

Her mind went all over the place. Were they headed to the coast? The mountains? They'd taken a honeymoon to Hawaii so maybe he was trying to recreate their memories by jetting off to their favorite resort.

"You'll never guess," he added with that sexy, crooked smile. "I can see your mind working, but we'll be there before you could ever think of what the destination is."

As the plane leveled out, Delilah unfastened

her belt and came to her feet with her glass. She needed to move, because even though their banter had been light, he was still right there. So close, so tempting. She wasn't naive. She knew this trip would bring about a repeat of the other night... which was still something they hadn't talked about.

"Have I been there before?" She turned back to face him as she crossed her arms and stared down at him. "Or is it some place we've been together?"

Camden laughed and shook his head. "We're not going to Hawaii and I'm not telling you anything else."

Delilah pursed her lips and tried like hell to think of where they'd be going. They both loved the beach, so she had a pretty good idea they would be heading to a coast, but which one? And they'd only decided this last night, so who had openings? Maybe a client of his had a rental?

"How did you find something on such short notice?" she asked.

He simply stared up at her and winked. That simple gesture was another punch of lust to her gut. He'd done that so many times over the years. When he held a secret that he wasn't about to let her in on, she merely got that wink. The combo with that naughty smile never failed to get another tug of arousal from her.

In his defense, her question had been ridiculous. If Camden wanted something, he got it. While he might have been raised with money and means, he didn't rely on his family name or his parents to obtain his goals. He'd become the best attorney to elite clients and had made a name for himself and his firm.

That determination and tenacity were just two of the qualities she'd fallen for when they'd met. They paralleled each other in so many ways, yet in the end, she knew if she stayed, they'd end up resenting each other. There were just too many negatives working against them.

Why did love and relationships have to be so damn difficult?

Camden patted the seat next to him. "Have a seat. You've got a little while before we land."

Delilah eyed him another moment before she crossed the narrow space and settled in once again. She fastened her belt back into place and took another sip of her wine. She might not know where they were going, but one thing was certain. This trip would most definitely be locked in her memory bank, and very likely her heart, for the rest of her life.

Six

The moment their driver pulled away from the home where he dropped them off, Camden turned his attention to Delilah. Her reaction coming over the bridge to the private island and up the tree-lined drive had been exactly what he'd thought. But now that they were standing in front of the pale blue two-story beach house, he wanted to see her delight.

When he'd first mentioned a getaway, he knew exactly where he'd take her if she agreed. Honestly, he'd started to give up hope that he'd ever get her here, but now his vision had become a reality.

Would she understand the meaning of this place? Should he even say anything? Maybe she wouldn't notice the special touches, but he hoped she did. He hoped she realized everything the place embodied.

"This house is beautiful," she exclaimed as her eyes seemed to travel over the second-story porch, then back down to the immaculate grounds. "Are we the only ones staying here?"

"We are."

She turned her attention to him and that megawatt smile that he'd missed so much now spread across her face. Damn, but she was gorgeous. She had such a natural beauty that he'd initially been drawn to. When he'd first met her at a mutual friend's wedding several years ago, there had been instant chemistry. One slow dance and a few glasses of wine later had been the start to their dynamic relationship and they'd been inseparable since.

Well, until several months ago when she insisted on moving out and demanding he file for divorce. He hadn't seen that coming and he would never forget that initial blow…or the lingering pain.

"Does this place belong to a client?" she asked.

Camden offered her a smile. "Something like that."

He reached for the handle of her bag and his, then nodded toward the entrance.

"Lead the way," he told her. "There's a code for the door."

She made her way up the decorative concrete path and his eyes were immediately drawn to her sexy, curvy frame. Following the sway of his wife's hips had been his favorite hobby for the past five years.

Cam gave her the code to enter and once again watched her face as the door swung open. The entire home had been remodeled and, per his orders, the kitchen had been well stocked for their visit…plus a few other little surprises.

He'd left strict orders for everyone to be gone before their arrival and for complete privacy during their stay. Camden wanted absolutely no distractions or outside interruptions coming between him and his wife…because she was still his wife and he'd fight for her to hold on to that title up until the very end.

"The inside is even more breathtaking than the outside," she gasped as she moved into the spacious open floor plan, placing her purse on the coffee table.

The wall of windows provided a stunning view of the calm ocean. The sun shone high in the sky, giving a sparkling effect on the crystal blue water. The bright light beaming through seemed to frame her in a beauty he hadn't considered before. He knew he'd wanted her here, he knew she'd love it if he could just get her to agree to come, but he hadn't taken into account how reality would impact him even more than the fantasy.

She belonged here. *They* belonged here.

"How on earth did you get this place on such short notice?" She spun around and faced him, but remained at the windows. "I mean, the view is gorgeous and the house is like something out of a magazine. If I lived here, I'd never leave. I'd have to find a way to change careers and work from home."

The pang in his chest only stemmed from regret. He had nobody to blame but himself for putting her in a position that made her feel like her only option was to leave. Marriages definitely took two people on the same page working just as hard as the other, but Camden was man enough to admit the majority of the blame for all the missteps along the way.

"You're in luck," he told her, ignoring the luggage and making his way across the room toward her. "You don't have to leave this house or the private beach, or even the island for the next four days. You can be as free as you want. We're the only ones around and I've made sure everything you could ever need is already here."

Delilah's eyes widened. "I have no clue how you did all of this in such a short time, but I'm impressed."

Camden stepped in front of her and barely resisted reaching out. He had to be patient. He had high hopes for these four days, but time was not on his side.

"There are definitely moments worth the sacrifice and extra work."

Her tongue darted out and swept across her bottom lip, stirring his desire even more. As if he needed any help in wanting his wife. Desire and passion were two of the main areas they excelled at.

"You really went all out for just four days," she murmured.

Camden shrugged. "Maybe there will be more than four days."

"You shouldn't get your hopes up," she told him. "This isn't a stepping-stone to some glossy future. This is our final trip together. We're making our last memories, Cam."

She might think that now, but he had plans to make her think differently. Some men might take that remark and just give up. Giving up wasn't even in Cam's vocabulary and he knew it wasn't in Dee's, either. They had something special and yes, they might be fighting outside forces, but that didn't mean it was time to call it quits or let anyone or anything else decide their future.

He wasn't going to argue with her, though. His actions would speak louder than any words ever could. And it was those actions, or lack of, over the past five years that had started crumbling their marriage—among other things. But, Camden could and would do his part. Maybe this was too little, too late, but he wanted his wife and he was damn well going to enjoy her during their time together.

"Are you hungry?"

Delilah stared at him, clearly taken aback by his change of topic.

"Um…not really. I wouldn't mind walking along the beach."

"Then let's get changed. I'll take your suitcase to your room."

"Aren't we sharing a room?"

That hope she'd told him not to get up suddenly rose even more. How could it not at her question? She'd assumed they'd be together sharing a bed like they always had…which is exactly what he wanted, but he would never force her or purposely make her uncomfortable.

Cam's heart kicked up as her dark eyes stared back at him. She always had the most expressive gaze, one any man could get lost in. He'd been a victim many times to that strong hold she had over him.

"I want nothing more than you in my room, but I also want you to feel like you're in control here."

"We're on a trip away together and we're still married…for now," she quickly amended. "Put my luggage in the same room as yours."

Before he could turn or even reply, his cell chimed from the pocket of her purse. She stared at him and had the audacity to grin. She might be enjoying this aspect a little too much, but he didn't mind. Whatever it took to show her he was serious, and he loved seeing her smile.

"Is that going to go off all the time while we're here?" she asked with a quirk of her brow.

Camden nodded. "Most likely. Feel free to silence it or just turn it off."

"Has this thing ever been turned off?" she asked, walking to the coffee table before pulling the ringing device from her purse.

She glanced at the screen and stilled, then blew out a sigh and turned the phone for him to see the screen.

His father.

"Answer it," she told him.

No way in hell was he answering. If there was a legitimate issue, his father would leave a message and he could call him back. Camden had always felt smothered as an only child, but he hadn't realized just how much his parents wanted, and tried, to control his life until he married Delilah. If he answered that phone, he would be putting Dee second once again and he had to make her feel certain that she was first in his life now.

But he had obligations and commitments. Taking an hour off was one thing, but four days was an entirely different situation. There were clients who would need him, though he'd told his assistant to take over while he was away. Not having access to the world he'd built did give him pause…but he had to do this. He promised Delilah he would. If he ever wanted a chance, now was the time to make that sacrifice.

Camden took the phone from her hand and declined the call before shutting the whole thing down. As he handed it back to her, he didn't miss the way her eyes widened in surprise or the way her mouth dropped as if she couldn't believe he'd just done that. Yeah, part of him couldn't believe it, either. Oddly enough, the move felt right.

"I meant it when I said these next few days were just for us," he informed her. "Now let's change and take that walk. I have some surprises for you later."

He hoped she was starting to see that he was changing, that he had actually changed and realized what was important. And he hoped like hell he didn't stumble along the way and screw everything up again.

Camden had told Delilah to change and meet him down on the beach. She had no idea what he was doing, but she'd thrown on her bikini and a lace cover-up, tossed a few things in her bag and headed that way. She followed the natural stone steps leading from the house to the sand and still had no idea how he managed to get a house on a private island all to themselves with virtually zero notice.

The man did have powerful friends and high contacts, so no doubt he just asked, but still…

"Perfect day to spend outside."

Delilah spun around as Camden crossed the path with a basket in hand. He'd also gotten more casual and showed up in a pair of navy board shorts and no shirt, leaving that well-defined chest on display. Of course she'd seen and touched every square inch of his body, but she never tired of taking in such beauty.

"What do you have there?" she asked, pointing to the basket.

"Just one of the many surprises I have in store for you." He started heading down the beach. "Follow me."

Intrigued, she fell in step beside him. Camden reached for her hand, something he hadn't typically done when they were together.

"What are you doing?" she asked.

"Romancing my wife."

Part of her wanted to scream that he should have done this for years, but the other part of her opened her heart just slightly, wanting to let him back in. He'd gone to so much trouble and did everything for her…for them. He was trying. He legit wanted her back, she had no doubt about that. His desire to hold on to her as his wife was never in question, but the reality of what they could and couldn't do was.

And just because he went to all this trouble and she was going to force herself to set aside all negative thoughts didn't mean things would work out in the end. Sweet romance and heated nights wouldn't make their foundation strong and they both knew it.

"I thought you brought me here just to have sex the whole time."

Camden's rich laugh had her smiling. "As much as I love the idea of you being naked for four days, even I need a break. Besides, we never just relax. We're both married to our jobs and never made time for anything else."

"One of us would have made the time," she corrected.

"That's a fair statement," he agreed. "My schedule and clients are demanding, but I am working on that. It won't be an overnight fix, but I'll get there."

She'd never even heard him discuss wanting to fix the problem. Up until she left, Camden never even admitted there was a problem. For him to be so open and willing to change…another part of her heart opened a little more.

"Through there." Camden pointed toward a little opening in a grove of cypress trees. "That's our spot."

Delilah ducked beneath a thick branch and fol-

lowed the sandy path toward the opening that re-
vealed a stunning cabana. The large thatched roof
shaded a white bed and two fat ottomans on either
side of a small table. One side of the cabana faced
the water just at the curve of the island.

"This is incredible," she exclaimed. "I know
we're in Georgia from the license plates we passed
on the highway getting here, but this reminds me
so much of Hawaii with the tropical vibes."

"The whole island is pretty remarkable," he
agreed as he sat the basket on the table. "We could
have had a little picnic on the beach, but I figured
you'd like this more."

She glanced up at the palm-style ceiling fan.
Clearly there had to be some solar power out here,
which made the secluded spot all the more amazing. The soft breeze slid through the open sides
and the subtle lull of the water relaxed her more
than she thought possible.

Delilah stared out at the ocean and wondered
when was the last time she'd had such a beautiful day.

"This view is breathtaking. I could stay here
all day."

"I agree."

She glanced at Camden, whose eyes were fixed
solely on her. There went that flip of her heart
once again…and Delilah had that tug of something
that went beyond physical. He'd always called her

beautiful or pretty and oftentimes sexy, but the way he could look at her and make her actually feel those things was a talent he possessed.

But this vulnerable gaze of his drew her to face him fully. Something about Cam seemed softer, and maybe it was the relaxed atmosphere, but perhaps it was more. She'd never quite seen this side of him and she wondered how long it would last.

A sliver of hope pushed through the fear inside her and she found herself taking one step, then another, until she stood before him. Cam reached up and tucked her hair behind her ears, never taking that intense gaze from her.

A lock of his dark hair blew across his forehead, but he never wavered. His fingertips trailed down her jawline, then her neck, then down the V of her cover-up. Delilah trembled, instinctively arching into his touch.

"You've always been so responsive," he murmured. "Just one touch sets you off."

Only his touch had that effect. She'd never come close to having anything like this with anyone else.

With his eyes still holding hers, he reached for the hem of her cover-up and eased it up. Slowly, the lacy garment swept over her head a second before he flung the unwanted article off to the side.

Delilah stood before him wearing only her two-piece blue bikini. She'd never been comfortable with her body and the extra pounds and dimples in her thighs, but she'd never felt anything but sexy when she was around Camden. He always had a way of making her feel like she was flawless, erasing any ugly thoughts she had about herself. Camden was definitely good for the self-esteem.

"Did you pack this skimpy suit for me?"

He outlined the triangles of her top with just one fingertip along her bare skin. Delilah's stomach knotted with arousal and anticipation. The man could draw out foreplay in the most delicious ways and make her nearly beg before he satisfied her.

"I packed it for myself," she corrected. "But if you want to enjoy the view, go right ahead."

A smile danced around his lips and she couldn't help but stare at that mouth that had pleasured her so many times over the years.

"Oh, I'm enjoying," he told her. "But it's served its purpose."

With an expert tug, he had the ties around her neck and behind her back undone, sending the scrap of strings to the floor. Cam then did the same with the ties on her hips. Delilah shifted to let the bottoms fall as well.

When she started to reach for Camden's shorts, he took a step back.

"No," he commanded. "Let me look at you. I need to see you in this light. So bare and beautiful. So amazingly perfect for me."

How could words be just as much of a turn-on

as his touch? Her body burned for him—she ached in a way that only Camden could elicit.

Delilah turned from him and slowly made her way over to the large bed in the middle of the cabana. The breeze whispered over her bare skin as she lay on her back, lifting up on her elbows to stare at him. But Camden was already in motion and the hunger in his eyes was unmistakable.

Her husband was about to have his way with her and she couldn't wait.

Seven

There was nothing Camden wanted more than for Delilah to remove his shorts, but he hadn't wanted to rush things. He meant it when he said he wanted to look at her, to take in all her beauty.

But the little minx had sashayed across the cabana and now lay on the bed tempting him with that sweet, curvy body. How the hell could he take things slow now?

An idea hit him and he turned to grab something from the basket on the table. If she wanted to play seductive games, she had met her match.

With a small container in hand, Camden crossed to the bed where she lay looking up at him with a soft smile on her face. He came to stand beside her and placed the container on the edge of the bed. After popping the lid, he reached inside for one fresh berry.

"Don't move," he ordered. "Watch."

He took one single berry and placed it between her breasts. Then he grabbed another, placing it just below the first. He continued this until he had a trail down her abdomen stopping just above her heat.

He glanced up to her face and her eyes met his. She continued to stare at him as he leaned down and plucked one berry between his teeth. One by one, he followed the trail with his mouth. He took his time, growing more aroused by the second. Delilah started squirming beneath him and he knew she was struggling just as much as he was.

Good. He wanted her aching and needy. He wanted her to crave his touch and her release. He needed her to want nobody else but him for anything.

He swallowed the last bite as he settled between her legs. Camden stared up her torso to find her looking down at him, her breathing heavy. He lifted both of her legs over his shoulders and smiled a second before he covered her core with his mouth.

Delilah cried out and that sound was the most beautiful he'd heard in a long time. He cupped her backside, lifting her even more so he could pleasure her. A second later, Delilah's hands were in his hair and her hips were jerking. He knew she was close. So close that he slid one finger into her and sent her over the edge.

She came undone around him and Camden relished her passion. This is exactly what he'd wanted from her. He'd wanted her to forget everything but them and just let go.

Once her trembling ceased, he came up on his knees and glanced down at her flushed body. Heavy-lidded eyes stared back up at him and she reached out.

"Now, Cam. I need you."

Physically, yes. But what about emotionally or long-term? When would she admit that?

Definitely a conversation for another time. Right now, he wanted nothing else to even enter his mind other than how to please his wife…and she'd clearly stated she needed him.

Camden joined their bodies and braced himself with his hands on either side of her face. Her ankles locked behind his back as her heels dug into him, urging him on. He needed more. There was never enough.

Leaning down, he captured her mouth with his. She threaded her fingers through his hair and returned the kiss. There was nothing like having his wife wrapped all around him and taking in all her desire.

But after satisfying her and watching her passion explode, Camden was barely hanging on here. He jerked faster and reached down to grip her hips, tipping her higher.

And that did it. She tore free of his kiss and cried out as her body bowed into his. Camden let himself go, gritting his teeth and straining to remain as close as possible to her. He didn't want this magical moment to end. He didn't want to leave this cabana or face anything that would be waiting for them after this getaway.

Camden eased to the side, cradling Delilah in his arms and pulling her with him. He came to lie on his back with her draped all over him. Her hair tickled the side of his face, but he didn't care. That used to annoy him, but now…he wasn't about to move.

"Do you have other tricks in that basket?" she asked after several moments of silence.

Camden laughed, trailing his fingers up and down her bare back. "All of that is food for us, but we're all out of the berries. Sorry about that."

She eased up and glanced down with a wide smile on her face. "Oh, you can eat all the food if that's what your plans are for it."

He loved seeing her this playful and relaxed. This is exactly what he'd had in mind when he brought her here.

She moved up even farther and straddled his lap as she stared around the cabana.

"Does this place remind you of Hawaii?" she asked. "I know I've said that, but there are just so many touches in the house and here that take me back."

That was the idea.

"There are several similarities," he agreed. "Do you like it here?"

Her attention jerked back to him. "Like it? I'm ready to live here, but I have a distillery I can't exactly pick up and move."

"You could always escape here on weekends or once a month for a reset," he suggested.

"That would get rather costly." She eased off his lap and off the bed. "Though I do think a recharge once a month isn't a bad idea. Even if it's just for a day. Elise, Sara and I have been going nonstop these past few years gearing up for this ten-year launch."

Camden sat up and watched as she grabbed her bikini and retied everything back into place. Such a shame to cover up the perfection, but having her strut around in that little two-piece sure as hell wasn't a bad view.

"You guys have done a remarkable job," he told her. "Even if I didn't know the owners and sleep with one of them, I'd still love the taste of the bourbon."

She faced him now with a wide smile. "We love hearing people praise our spirits. We worked hard on all of it from the taste to the packaging. I'm just glad the ten-year is out and we can breathe a little sigh of relief. I'm hoping that leads to more anticipation when we reveal our fifteen and twenty in the future."

The bourbon process was rather lengthy, but Delilah wasn't one to give up on anything. When she wanted something, she worked too hard to keep it.

Which was why having her move out had hurt so damn bad. He knew she left in part for his sake. He knew she left in some attempt to set him free so he'd be happy in the long run and to keep the relationship between him and his parents secure.

To hell with all of that. He was the one who should be the protector, but how the hell could he protect Delilah from herself?

Camden slid off the bed and went to grab his shorts. He didn't want to bring up any topic that would remind her of what they were fighting against.

"Do you want to have a picnic in here or take it out to the beach?" he asked.

She pursed her lips and glanced out toward the ocean then back to him. "Definitely outside. I love the mountain views where we live, but I want to be on the beach as much as I possibly can while we're here."

"I figured you'd say that." He picked up the basket and gestured for her to lead the way. "You've always loved the water. That's something we'll make a point to add into our schedules."

When she opened her mouth, no doubt to argue, Camden held a hand up. "Don't say it. Let's just enjoy the day."

She closed her mouth and nodded. Relief spread through him that she didn't have a comeback about this being their final trip. Maybe they were making progress or maybe she was just appeasing him. Either way, this was a victory and he was going to ride this high for the next few days.

After that, well…only time would tell what their future held.

"Maybe sunscreen should be packed next time."

Delilah stared at Cam's broad, bare shoulders in the reflection of the mirror. The en suite bath was something from a magazine. The spacious room could have been plucked straight from her mind. Every single thing in here was exactly her taste from the freestanding bathtub inside the monstrous shower to the chandelier over the makeup vanity area to the white chaise in front of the massive walk-in closet.

"I'd take a little sunburn if it meant spending the day with you like we did." His eyes met hers in the mirror. "I wouldn't change a thing."

Yeah, she wouldn't, either. The lovemaking, the

picnic, playing in the water…there was so much that had happened. So many memories had been made in just this first day. She'd certainly seen a different side of Camden, and he hadn't mentioned his cell or his work one time. He truly seemed at peace and completely comfortable decompressing.

While she on the other hand had a mountain of anxiety coursing through her. All of the what-ifs kept bumping into one another inside her head.

What if she tried to go back and things worked out? What if they didn't? What if today was a glimpse into the future they could have? But what if it was just a temporary thing?

No matter what question popped into her head, another one came right on the coattails to counteract it.

Why couldn't he have done all of this before? Because doing it all now almost made her wonder if he was just afraid of failing or if he actually loved her.

Before she could say anything, her cell chimed from the bedroom. She hesitated, but Camden smiled.

"We never said you couldn't answer your phone," he joked.

Delilah laughed as she went through to the bedroom. She'd left her cell charging on one of the nightstands and spotted Sara's name on the screen. She waited, wondering if she should answer or just let it go to voice mail. After losing Milly, she usually answered everything, but now, well, she didn't want to get into a conversation about where she was or who she was with.

"Aren't you going to answer that?"

Delilah glanced over her shoulder at Camden, who stood in the wide doorway wearing nothing but a towel. Her eyes raked down his bare chest and to the knot securing the towel he held at his side.

"I'm thinking," she replied. "Are you getting in the shower?"

"If you keep looking at me like that, I won't make it to the shower."

Her eyes darted back up to his and the ringing finally stopped. The silence surrounded them, the sexual tension enveloped them.

"Who are you dodging?" he asked.

"Sara."

He nodded and, without a word, he released the towel. The white terry pooled around his feet as he simply continued to stare and smirk her way. That man knew what he was doing. He knew she'd never been able to turn down his advances. That's precisely why she'd fled the back room at the Angel's Share gala when he'd kissed her. If he'd even attempted to touch her in any other way, she would have jerked him into her office, locked the door and said to hell with her duties.

"Are you calling her back or joining me?"

Her cell chimed again, indicating a voice mail. If Sara left a message, there must be something important. She pulled her attention from temptation and tapped on her phone, putting the message on speaker.

"Hey, sis." Sara's chipper voice came through the cell. "I know you're on sabbatical, but I wanted to let you know I talked to the PI I hired and she might have some leads on my father, and I wanted to know if you wanted—"

Dee paused the message and regretted putting it on speaker. She would listen to the rest later in private, but clearly there wasn't an emergency. She risked turning back around and seeing the look on Cam's face.

He looked exactly how she thought he would... confused. With those dark brows drawn in and arms crossed over his chiseled chest, the man looked like he wanted some answers.

"How about that shower?" she suggested as she started back across the room.

When she stood before him, he took hold of her shoulders and gently squeezed.

"Want to tell me what that was about?" he asked.

Part of her did want to tell him, but the other part was afraid of opening up that aspect of her life if Cam wasn't going to be part of her future. Her thoughts were so damn muddled, she figured she should err on the side of caution rather than blurting out the truth followed by all her fears.

"Not now," she replied.

A sliver of hurt flashed through his eyes, but it was gone in an instant. She knew he wanted her to share her life, but if they did indeed divorce, she couldn't keep him in all her loops. Once that divorce was final, all ties would be severed and tying up another one would only keep them bound even longer. There had to be an actual end for both of them to move on.

"We agreed not to discuss anything outside of us and here, right?" she asked.

Delilah didn't wait for a reply as she reached for the hem of her sundress and pulled it up and over her head. She didn't have a stitch of clothing beneath and her nakedness quickly distracted Camden.

His lips thinned, his eyes traveled over her and his arousal was impossible to ignore.

"You're trying to change the subject," he murmured.

She reached for him and started backing him into the en suite and toward the tile-and-glass shower built for a party.

"It's working." She smiled. "You don't care about that phone call when you have other, more important things on your mind."

"There's only one important part of my life and she's always on my mind."

That bold statement warmed her, and her heart started healing…she only hoped it didn't break again. How could he shatter her and then attempt to rebuild? She couldn't let this happen. Anything outside of physical could damage her once again, and the fear that curled through her was very real and very scary.

Before she could travel down that maudlin path, Camden gripped her waist and lifted her off the ground. She squealed from the shock, but laughed as he carried her into the shower and immediately turned on all the sprays. The two rain heads and side jets pelted her as she wrapped her arms and legs around Camden's body. He adjusted the temperature, thankfully making the chilled water warmer.

Then Delilah found her back against the tile at the same time his body joined hers. Everything happened so fast, yet so perfectly. Delilah used the wall as leverage to move her body against his. Water sluiced all around them and her hair clung to her shoulders and onto his arms.

When Delilah's eyes met his, her breath caught in her throat. Cam's dark stare held hers with an intensity she hadn't seen too often. The way he moved combined with that passionate glare had her body climbing.

This was how they were, though. Intimacy could be fast and powerful or calm and gentle. No matter how he made love to her, Delilah always felt cherished.

Didn't that count for something? He showed her in so many ways how he felt and maybe she'd misunderstood the way he showed his love.

But being cherished didn't mean the man had completely changed. It only meant he didn't want to lose and he was fulfilling that promise to make these the most relaxing four days.

But four days wouldn't erase all the neglect and hurt from their past.

"Stay with me, Dee," he murmured as he leaned in closer. "Stop thinking, stay right here where we both need to be."

He was right. She had to get out of her head, at least for the moment.

Delilah framed his face with her hands and captured his lips. She loved kissing him, she loved having his hands all over her as she grew closer to her release. There were times she simply couldn't get enough and being without him for seven months only heightened her need. The other night in the car and earlier at the beach had only whet her appetite for her husband.

Cam slid his hands between their bodies and touched her where they joined…sending her body soaring. She closed her eyes and moaned as her climax slammed into her. Her knees tightened against his sides and his hips jerked even faster, drawing out her pleasure.

Within seconds, Camden stilled and tensed as he

let himself go. She clung to him, wanting to feel every bit of his release. He dropped his head to her shoulder and pressed her a little harder against the tile.

Moments later, he eased back and brought his head up.

"Did I hurt you?"

Delilah smoothed that dark, damp hair from his forehead. "Not at all."

"Damn. I should have taken my time, but…"

"Yeah, but…"

Their desire was stronger now than ever. Those words didn't need to be said aloud they were both so aware. She could think of little else.

"Do you want to talk?" he asked, helping her to stand on her own feet.

"About what?"

He spun her so the spray wasn't right in her face and slid his thumb across her bottom lip. "That phone call earlier."

Delilah chewed on the inside of her cheek and glanced away.

"Hey." He cupped her face and turned her attention back to him. "No matter what happens or the outcome with us, I still care. I always will. You can trust me with whatever is going on."

"You haven't always stood up for me or made it clear I can trust that you'll be there."

The muscle in his jaw clenched and he waited a beat before he answered. Dee wondered if she went too far, but those words needed to be said. Hiding her feelings for years certainly hadn't helped this relationship.

"I never want my trust to be in question." He stroked her bottom lip as he continued to hold her gaze. "I mean it when I say I've changed and that you are the main priority in my life. No matter what, I need you to know that and the only way for you to realize is for my actions to back up my words."

Those actions hadn't been backed up before, so only time would tell if they would now. She knew in his heart he was sincere, but she also knew that outside this little getaway bubble they were in, real life would likely consume him once again. Not to mention, if they went their separate ways, she couldn't keep depending on him as her sounding board. She had to stand on her own two feet and work through her own issues without Camden.

For the first time in months, she wondered if she should stay and try to make this all work...but she also shouldn't be making any postcoital decisions regarding her marriage and her future.

Eight

Delilah padded her way from the bedroom and down the hall. She hadn't explored the house since arriving yesterday. She'd been a little busy enjoying herself, but her stomach growled and Camden was still sleeping so she figured she'd find the kitchen and get breakfast started.

She passed by the living room, pausing for just a moment to appreciate the breathtaking view once again. She figured the kitchen had to be off the living room and she was right. This room might just be the showstopper. The rest of the house was incredible, but this oversize eat-in kitchen would sell the house. Whoever owned this property was one lucky guy.

There was a wall of glass doors that would open

to allow the space to be one big entertainment area. The covered patio had cushy sofas and hanging chairs with lush plants all around. And the infinity pool that overlooked the ocean was another upscale added bonus.

Delilah made her way toward the large center island. There were stools around three sides to accommodate plenty of guests. Who needed a home this large? Whoever it was clearly had a big family or they just loved living the high life with lavish things.

When she turned to find where the coffee was located, she spotted a gorgeous bundle of flowers in the window above the sink.

Hibiscus and they were fresh. Another added touch from the people who rented out this place.

The flowers with the ocean in the background had her once again thinking of her honeymoon. Camden had given her a pink hibiscus each evening for her to put in her hair before they went to dinner. She couldn't help the smile that spread across her face as she stared at the blooms.

This trip was exactly what she needed and she was so glad she decided to meet Cam at the airport. There was still that fear inside, though, that all of this was temporary. She'd come on this trip dead set on having a fling with him and making this their final goodbye, but she was so torn. If their life could be like this all the time, maybe there was hope. Maybe they stood a chance. Granted this was a mini-vacation and things couldn't always be sunshine and rainbows in any relationship, but now that they both saw how good things could be…could there be a future?

There was still that issue of his parents' disapproval, and Camden wanted a family. She had her own family drama going on right now with discovering her adoptive sisters were actually biological half sisters and that their adoptive mom, Milly, was in fact their aunt. Her own family had solidified even more and even though the revelation had caught her off guard, she felt even closer to her sisters. She wanted that personal, intimate connection with Cam and she'd always assumed whomever she married, she would also have that tight bond with her in-laws. Unfortunately, the opposite had been true.

Delilah rubbed her head as she searched for coffee in the pantry. According to documents they'd uncovered in Milly's house after her passing, Delilah, Elise and Sara's birth mother had been an addict and ultimately passed while in prison. Milly had shielded them from the hurt and sought them out as toddlers to adopt all three. Milly had been a saint to be a single mother of three young girls, but she'd made everything look so easy.

And now Delilah had the choice whether to look for her biological father or let it go. Originally she didn't want more disruptions in her life, but now she wanted to know where she came from. She wanted to know her heritage. Her mother had been white, so Dee clearly got her darker skin and hair from her father. Did she look like him? Did she have other siblings she didn't know about?

Elise had decided not to search for her father, but Delilah and Sara were both interested enough to want to do some digging. Delilah wasn't sure what she would do with the information if and when she found the man.

It was all still too much to take in. Every change in her life seemed to explode all at once lately and she could only deal with one crisis at a time. Which was the exact reason this trip and the serene setting did wonders for her frazzled nerves and battered heart.

"Are you going to stand in front of the pantry until breakfast appears?"

Startled, Delilah spun around, her hand to her heart. "I thought you were sleeping."

Camden rubbed his bare chest as he walked into the kitchen and glanced around. "I was, but I typically don't sleep in so this was a change."

"I remember," she told him. "You were always up and out the door before I even had my first cup of coffee."

He came to stand in front of her and leaned in

for a quick kiss. "I should have stuck around and had a cup with you."

Considering they could do nothing to change the past, she didn't want to get into the "could have" or "would have" scenarios.

"You can have that cup now," she offered. "Do you know where things are? I assume you've been here before?"

"I've been here a few times," he admitted. "Go sit out on the patio and I'll whip up something for us."

Delilah laughed. "You're going to cook breakfast?"

Clearly offended, Cam crossed his arms over his chest and raised a dark brow. "How hard can it be?"

"Well, don't let me stop you." She patted his cheek and offered a smile. "I'll take my coffee first, if you don't mind."

As she started to skirt around him, Cam snaked an arm out and around her waist, pulling her back against his side. His eyes held her in place and that desire started brewing once again.

"I don't take orders very well," he murmured. "But, considering you're standing here wearing my shirt and looking sexy as hell, I'll allow it."

She'd tossed on his shirt and nothing else before she'd left the bedroom. She wasn't trying to be sexy, more like trying to be quiet so she didn't wake him, and his simple white tee was the closest thing she'd reached for. But if this would get her added perks, she'd be wearing nothing else the rest of this trip.

Delilah opened the sliding glass doors all the way to let the morning breeze in. Everywhere she went on this property, whether inside the house, the cabana or on the private beach, kept her wishing she could stay here. But, this wasn't her home—it was just an amazing vacation. She wondered how much this went for and if she could get it for her and her sisters to have a girls' trip sometime. They could all use a break if leaving the distillery at the same time would even be a possibility.

She settled into the corner of one of the sectional sofas and propped her feet up. She'd have to take advantage of that pool tonight. Swimming beneath the stars, or better yet, skinny-dipping, had quite the appeal.

Something crashed in the kitchen, quickly followed by a string of cursing. Delilah merely smiled and decided to let Cam figure it all out. She kind of liked him taking charge and looking after things. She'd never been one to relinquish control, but if he wanted to do this for her, she wasn't about to argue.

Him wanting to care for her was sweet. Oh, he'd said that's what he wanted to do all along, but that version of caring and this were totally different. She didn't need to be cared for financially—she needed care for her soul. She needed that emotional support more than she needed anything else.

Could Camden really be that guy now? Did her leaving and filing for divorce give him some sort of wake-up call? She hadn't even thought that possible. She truly didn't know what to expect or think when she'd left. All she knew was that she couldn't stay any longer. The longer she stayed, the more that tension and resentment would grow. She loved him too much to have him resent her down the road. There was also an unhealthy amount of resentment from her side. The times when Cam could have stood up for her, been there for her, he hadn't. Now he wanted to rectify all of that and she truly believed that's what he thought he could do, but only time would tell and she didn't know if she had more to give.

Delilah still didn't see how everything could work between them. A few days in paradise on a secluded island wouldn't solve their problems, but this did make her see that she still loved him. She enjoyed their time together if their time could always be like this…with a caring, thoughtful husband who put their marriage above all else. Oh, she knew any relationship had bumps and dips, but she had grown tired of going up against the only people in his life. His parents had gone so far as labeling her a "gold digger" when she and Cam married and they'd stuck by that even though she'd proved that she could stand on her own.

Milly had instilled independence and strength in each of the girls. Having her gone was definitely a void, but her spirit and legacy lived on and Delilah wanted to make her proud. Milly had always loved Camden and believed Dee and Cam belonged together. When they separated Milly assured her that she and Cam would work it out. Delilah could sure use some advice right now from the sweetest lady she'd ever known.

Two monumental moments in her life had collided—Milly's death and the impending divorce—and Delilah wasn't sure how to grieve, quite honestly. Her emotions seemed to be torn in all directions and the fear that she was doing everything wrong was a real threat.

"Fresh coffee, a splash of unsweetened almond milk, and sugar-free vanilla syrup."

Delilah shifted her attention to Camden, who stood before her presenting her with her favorite coffee. She reached for the steaming mug and inhaled the robust aroma.

"I'm impressed you had my coffee order items delivered here," she told him as she took a sip.

"Impressing you is my new mission," he stated. "It should have been my mission all along, but I took you for granted and assumed you'd always be around."

Delilah gripped the warm mug with both hands and blinked up at him. "It's just coffee, Cam. It's okay."

"It's not okay," he countered. "It's these little things that you needed, that I recognize now."

He raked a hand down his jawline; the coarse hair of his beard bristled against his palm. He struggled, that much was evident, but she hadn't realized just how much so. All this time she'd been thinking about her pain, her problems, but Camden had been experiencing his own anguish.

Cam moved and sank onto the edge of the sofa next to her hip. He stared out at the water and she waited for him to grapple with his thoughts. She didn't know if he was going to share anything or if he just needed a moment. Either way, she was here.

And maybe that's what he needed. She'd been wanting him to be there for her emotionally, but had she been there for him?

Damn. Had she been selfish this entire time?

"It's so ridiculous," he muttered with a soft laugh. "The day after you left, I went into our bathroom to get ready for work and it hit me. I stared at that stupid bath mat and cursed everything because I missed seeing your tiny footprints on there."

Delilah nearly upended her coffee at his vulnerable statement. She'd never heard him admit anything so sweet, so from the heart. Did all of this stem from him wanting to win or did he legitimately want to expose his true self and emotions?

She placed her hand on his thigh. "Cam—"

A buzzer from the kitchen went off and Camden came to his feet. The moment passed, but it would forever live inside of her. His admission healed something in her own heart, a piece that had been shattered. But the fact he'd been so open with her was another layer of balm that soothed her pain.

How could they just move on to breakfast and a normal day after this? He'd exposed a piece of himself. He'd never been that open before in all their years of marriage. She didn't want to gloss over this or not recognize how important this was for him…for them.

Trust had to be a key player in any relationship from here on out. If she'd discovered anything recently, that was certainly it. Milly had lied, though her reasoning was justified on her part, but still, the sting of that betrayal continued to linger. She had to trust that Cam was doing all of this for her for the right reasons and not just because he hated failing. There was more to a marriage than just winning.

Delilah sat her mug on the accent table and came to her feet. As she made her way into the kitchen, she couldn't help but laugh as Cam waved a kitchen towel through the smoke over the stove and turned on the exhaust fan.

Another string of curses had her laughing even harder. Camden glanced over his shoulder and sighed.

"I hope you like your bacon well-done."

"It's my favorite."

Who knows. Maybe vulnerable admissions and burnt breakfasts were their new beginning. Maybe this was a chance at something new and they could work on seeing how they could maneuver this life together, because the only way to do that would be to start over.

This vacation wasn't just a respite for her mind and spirit but a fresh start for their entire future… if she could trust everything happening here.

Nine

"So tell me about this guy Elise is engaged to."

Camden sat on the second-story porch just off the main bedroom. He'd tucked himself in the corner of the sofa and Delilah had sat at the other end with her legs extended along the cushions, her bare feet propped in his lap.

"Antonio is amazing and they are so perfect together," she told him, her voice dreamier than usual. "He's so supportive of her and she's the same for him. He'd come from his small town in Spain to do some tours of vineyards and distilleries for his family's restaurants. He and Elise got locked in the cellar of the castle and apparently fell in love."

Camden laughed as he slid his thumb up the

arch of her foot and back down. They'd been out here since the sun went down and their wineglasses had been emptied, but neither was ready to get up. He was fine with that. The longer he had her relaxed and talking, the more hopeful he felt that she was coming around.

"That's quite a meet story," he replied. "I take it he's moving here?"

"He's going to be doing a great deal of traveling, but they will mostly be in Kentucky. They're getting married at the castle. It will be our first major event and we're planning to open it up for more after that."

Camden nodded in agreement at the idea. "That sounds like a brilliant business plan. Turning an old historic castle into a distillery was your first excellent move. You guys have really tapped into something magical."

"We have, but if the product isn't good, then nothing we do will matter," she explained. "I'm just glad we have that great gin that we were able to slide into the industry while we waited on the bourbon to age in the barrels."

"You're so damn sexy when you talk business."

Delilah laughed and leaned forward to swat at his shoulder. "You always say that."

"It's true," he defended, moving to stroke her other foot. "That intelligent mind of yours is just one of the reasons I fell so hard for you. You and your sisters were already in the process of perfecting your bourbon, you had the castle and had just finished renovating and then opened it to the public for tours. You were talking about the process of how to bottle and the goals you all had. It was amazing to watch you check each one off your list."

Delilah tipped her head and rested it against the cushion. The stars shone bright tonight with the full moon. The subtle sound of the waves relaxed him even more. What if he'd taken her away on a trip like this from the start of their marriage? What if, instead of working his ass off to prove to her he could care for her, he actually showed her?

"I know your parents think I was struggling with Angel's Share, but—"

"No."

There was no way in hell he was going to let any negativity ruin their peaceful evening.

"No matter what they believe, then or now, I know the truth. I never once thought you were using me."

"I've discovered how important family truly is," she went on. "Especially lately. And the idea of continuing to be that barrier between you guys really guts me. Milly's death just drove home that our separation was the right thing to do. At the end of the day family is really all you have and can fulfill a piece of you that no career could do."

He released her foot and shifted until he faced her. He eased in closer and rested his hand on her thigh.

"Listen," he urged. "Everything going on between my parents and me started long before you. I didn't realize it until we married. They've been controlling all of my life and I didn't know any better but to let them. So when I defied everything they wanted from me, they didn't know what to do and you took the brunt of their anger. But I had dealt with them for so long that I never took what they said to heart. I now realize that you did."

He paused, then replayed her comment in his mind. Something niggled at him, something that he wanted her to open up about. He wanted, needed her to trust him with everything if this was going to work. How else could they move on? Because he knew she was thinking about it. Delilah wanted this just as much as he did...but she was afraid and it was his job to make her feel secure.

He suddenly had new goals for this marriage, and he took his jobs very seriously. Now he just had to figure out how the hell to juggle it all because failure in any aspect of his life was not acceptable.

"You said you realized the importance of family, especially lately," he reminded her. "The loss of Milly is a big part of that, but is there more?

Maybe something that has to do with Sara's phone call last night?"

Delilah stared at him for a moment before turning her attention out toward the ocean. Camden waited. While he wanted to know, he also didn't want to push her to where she wasn't comfortable.

"Sara found some letters," Dee stated, still staring out into the starry night. "Old letters and documents in Milly's house last month. We found out that we are actually biological sisters."

"What?"

She faced him once again. "Well, half sisters."

"Dee, that's amazing."

He stroked her leg and inched even closer at this shocking news. The three of them had always been so close, like best friends raised as sisters, but to know they had some of the same genes— that was such a shock.

"That's what Sara called about," Delilah went on. "She wants to find her biological father. Elise said she's happy the way her life is and she's not interested in looking."

"What about you?"

"At first I didn't want to because life was chaotic enough, but after thinking about it, I want to know where I came from," she told him. "I want to know if I look like my father or if I have other siblings. But then I think like Elise and I'm happy with the family I have, and do I want to disrupt someone else's life? He might not want to know he has a child somewhere, or on the other hand, maybe he knew about me and didn't want me."

Camden's heart clenched. He couldn't imagine all the thoughts and doubts swirling through her mind. Add all she'd been dealing with regarding their marriage and Milly's death...

"Do you know anything about your biological mother?" he asked.

Delilah nodded and sat up straighter, pulling her legs in and crossing them. Clearly the topic had her on edge and unnerved. He didn't blame her. He had no idea what was going on in her head right now. This was a bomb of information that she likely was still trying to process.

"She was Milly's sister, actually," Dee finally stated. "Our mom was an addict and went to prison so we were placed in foster care. Long story short, Milly tracked us down and adopted us. Our mother ended up dying in prison so I never knew her, never even saw a picture of her."

Even with the constant friction with his own parents, Camden couldn't imagine never knowing either of them or having one taken away. There was no common ground here or any possible way he could fathom what she was going through. Having someone listen who wasn't one of her sisters would be the best thing for Dee right now.

"My thoughts are all over the place," she went

on. "Some days I want to know who my father is and other days I think it's best I don't. I know Milly was protecting us, but was that because this was so much to handle, or maybe our fathers were not good people. I just don't know. I do think that if I had the information, I'd have a little relief, you know? Like, everything is there and if I decide I need to reach out, then I can."

"That makes sense," he assured her. "You would have the control that way and some of your life will be back in your hands."

She offered a soft smile and tipped her head. "You get it. I wasn't sure what you'd say or even if I was going to tell you."

He reached out and took her hand, giving a gentle squeeze. "I'm glad you did. Have you talked to Sara since she left that message?"

Delilah shook her head. "The girls don't know about this trip. I just told them I was off the grid for a while and would see them in the office when I get back."

Camden didn't like the lump of fear that settled in him. He knew why Elise and Sara didn't know about Dee's plans. She wasn't ready to tell them anything was going on. She'd told him coming in that this was a final trip, their last goodbye and their final memories together.

But he'd thought for sure she'd started coming around. He knew Delilah so well and there wasn't a doubt in his mind that she was thoroughly enjoying herself and finally releasing some of her stress. Of course, he'd had no idea just how much she'd been holding in.

"Whatever you decide, I want you to know you can count on me," he told her. "I'll support you or give you advice. Anything you need."

She blinked and the moonlight caught the shimmer of unshed tears in her eyes.

"This," she murmured. "This is what I need. Just for you to be present in the moment, to listen to me. You don't know how many times I wanted that. I *needed* it."

The guilt of all those years of not opening his eyes and paying attention weighed heavy on him. He couldn't change the past, but he could sure as hell change the present and future. He had to prove to Delilah that she was just as important as his career and family. But trying to put everything in that first place slot was going to be damn difficult.

Without a word, Camden eased her legs aside and came to his feet. He bent down and scooped her up into his arms, cradling her against his chest as he carried her back into the house. She rested her head against his shoulder and sniffed. The only time he'd seen her cry in all their years together was at Milly's graveside. Even though they'd split, he still had to be there to offer his support. Not to mention he'd loved Milly, too.

But even when Delilah had told him she was leaving, she hadn't shed a tear. She'd been stony and strong and determined. That was his Delilah. She'd always been so resilient, but there was only so much any person could take. He never wanted to see her break, and he knew she'd never admit she needed help or might be falling apart, but he was glad he was the one here.

Cam moved over to the bed and gently lay Delilah down before crawling in beside her and pulling her into his arms. She nestled against him, her hands clutching his T-shirt as if holding on for a lifeline.

"I'm not going anywhere," he murmured against her forehead. "I'm always here. No matter what."

He just hoped like hell she would always be there, too.

"What now?" Delilah asked, following Cam's lead down to the beach toward the cabana area. "You don't even have the basket. Did you forget the fruit?"

He smiled as he reached back for her hand.

"I didn't forget anything," he assured her. "Everything is down here."

They had one more day left and she was not ready to see their time here come to an end. The way Camden had comforted her last night, held her and soothed her pain...that was so much more than she'd ever thought she'd receive from him.

Her heart had flipped. Camden had turned over something within her he'd never done before and the connection had absolutely nothing to do with intimacy or sex. He'd been the rock she didn't know she'd been needing. She knew she'd wanted him mentally present, but she didn't realize that she'd started to crumble until he'd picked her up and carried her to bed. They hadn't made love, he'd simply held her.

Who knew absolutely no words would be the key to starting that healing process?

"Stop here."

Delilah came to a stop at his command and glanced around.

"What am I supposed to be doing?" she asked.

"Close your eyes."

She jerked back and shook her head. "Oh, no. I'm not closing my eyes. You know I don't like surprises."

He shielded her eyes with his hand. "You love them. We've already been over this. Now just let me do this for you."

She sighed and obeyed, but that didn't mean she had to like it. That whole fear of the unknown always sucked the fun out of the actual surprise, but she was learning to relax...or at least she was trying. So far everything Cam had done for her had been absolutely spectacular. He'd spoiled her in every single way.

Was this really the new Camden? Was her husband turning into the person she'd needed? If he was, was there even a possibility they could forge a deeper bond and overcome the issue that his parents caused? Trust was something that had to build over time and much more than four days allowed for. But she was seeing a change, she was seeing his efforts, and that had to count for something… right?

"I'll cooperate, but only because you've done so well with the surprises," she joked.

Camden's laughter had her smiling. One large hand covered her eyes and the other took her hand and led her through the soft sand.

"There's nothing in front of you but me," he assured her. "Just keep coming. We're going inside the cabana, so I'll tell you where the steps are."

He led her carefully and she trusted him completely. How could she not? Camden really did have her best interest at heart and he seemed to be thriving in growing their bond even though she'd told him this wasn't a stepping-stone into their future. The man wasn't giving up and everything about that attitude was sexy as hell.

Camden guided her into the cabana with ease and then he released her.

"Open your eyes."

Delilah blinked and took in the sights. Two ladies stood beside large white tables. Soft music filled the open space and there were fresh pink hibiscus all around the place. In vases, lining the floor to the tables, across the bed.

She turned her attention to Cam, who merely smiled at her.

"You can't relax without having a nice massage," he told her. "I remember how much you loved them."

From their honeymoon. They'd gotten a massage every single day.

But this…this was all so amazing. He'd managed to get people onto the island and all set up and she'd had no clue.

"You went to a great deal of trouble for this," she murmured.

Cam merely shrugged and gestured toward the tables and smiled. "No trouble at all and you need this."

That she could definitely agree with. She had no idea if Cam finagled this all this morning after her mini-meltdown last night or if he had this day planned all along. Regardless, he knew exactly what she needed. This wasn't just a getaway; this entire trip was an awakening.

"Hello, my name is Ann and this is Carey," one of the masseuses said. "We'll step out while you two undress and get under the sheets. Then we'll get started on your deep tissue massages."

As they stepped out, Delilah turned to Camden and threw her arms around his neck. She smacked a kiss on his lips and eased back.

"You're going to make this very difficult to leave here," she told him.

His hands went to her backside and he gripped the material of her sundress and started pulling it up. She shifted so he could pull the garment over her head.

She'd put her swimsuit on beneath because she'd had no clue what they were going to be doing.

"New suit?" he asked, his eyes raking over her.

"I've had it a year or so, just never had a reason to wear it. There's not exactly been opportunities, working fourteen hours a day and gearing up for the bourbon launch."

He reached behind her neck and untied the red halter top, then went to her back and did the same.

"You look amazing in red," he muttered as his fingertips trailed over her bare breasts. "Maybe I should send the ladies away and work on you myself."

"Let's let them do their thing and then you can do what you want later," she proposed. "I'll even wear the red if you want."

He dropped to his knees and started sliding the

bottoms down her legs. "Oh, I want," he stated, staring up at her.

Once she was completely undressed, she had to move toward one of the tables before she forgot about the women and let her husband have his way.

"They're going to come back in soon and you're not going to be ready." Delilah climbed onto the table and covered her bottom half with the sheet. "Better hurry so we can get to our own private plans later."

He kept his dark eyes on hers and reached behind his neck to grab his T-shirt. He jerked it over his head and then eased his shorts down. He took them and all of her clothes and placed them on an accent table before coming back to the tables.

Once he lay on the one next to hers, he reached across and took her hand.

"You belong here," he told her. "Just like this. Beauty surrounded by beauty. I'm glad you came with me."

Yeah, she was, too. The ladies came back in before she could answer. Delilah simply squeezed his hand in response and couldn't wait until they could be alone again.

Ten

"Just let me retire here and tell my sisters to visit."

Camden laughed and stared at Delilah's back. She stood at the edge of the balcony off their bedroom, staring out at the sunset, with the wind blowing through her hair. She wore some little pair of shorts that barely covered her backside and a tank that didn't quite cover her midsection. She was breathtaking and now more than ever, he wanted her to fight for this, for them, because he wasn't about to give up.

"There's no reason we can't come back," he told her.

He remained in the open doorway from the bedroom, leaning against the jamb. He could stand here all evening and watch her as she enjoyed the private island and all its beauty. This was exactly how he'd imagined her and everything she'd needed to start to heal. They both had healing to do, but his sole purpose right now was succeeding with this marriage.

Her hair whipped in the wind as she glanced at him over her shoulder.

"Will there be a chance for us to come back?" she asked.

This was tricky. Every moment with her could make or break their future. But he had to be honest and he had to lay everything on the line.

"We can come here any time you want, Dee. I own the island and the house."

Her eyes widened as she turned to face him completely. Silence settled between them and she continued to just stare.

"I bought this place right before you moved out," he went on when she still said nothing. "I had plans for you and I coming here to renovate, but then you left and I had the changes made with you in mind."

Delilah took one step, then another. With her eyes locked onto his, she slowly closed the distance between them.

"You own all of this?" she asked. "And you're just now telling me?"

"I was going to surprise you, but then you packed and left," he defended. "So at that point I didn't want to say I did this and have you think I only did it to get you back. I had plans in motion before you ever moved out. But then as time went on, I knew I wanted to surprise you after everything was complete. I was seriously hoping you didn't see this property listed in the original divorce agreement."

She continued to stare in disbelief. The gentle ocean breeze lifted strands of her dark hair and slid them across her face. Camden reached out and smoothed the wayward pieces behind her ears and framed her face.

"All I could think was how happy you were on our honeymoon," he went on, gliding his thumb over her bottom lip. "You looked so beautiful each night with the flower in your hair. You would smell it each time before you put it in."

"That's why there's been hibiscus here," she murmured. "How did you get all of this done, though?"

Camden shrugged. "I placed a few phone calls."

"What would you have done had I not shown up at your hangar?"

Cam laughed. "I would have enjoyed a massage and all the food I had stocked, I guess."

She looped her arms around his neck and smiled. "I can't believe you bought an island for us."

"I had to do something," he replied. "I was losing you… I *lost* you."

Delilah blinked and bit down on her bottom lip

for a second before she let out a sigh and leaned her forehead against his.

"Part of me thinks there's no way we can get past the fact your parents never accepted me, and I don't want to be the person who keeps you guys in turmoil," she told him. "I still worry that your job will come before me and that you won't see me as an equal in this. I can take care of myself, but I need you by my side, not three steps in front of me trying to pave the way."

Camden tipped her head back and leaned in even more, his mouth hovering just above hers. "And what about the other part of you?"

Her lids lowered as she feathered her lips across his.

"The other part wants to be selfish and naive and pretend this marriage isn't in trouble." She trailed her lips down and across his jawline. "I want to live in this fantasy world you've created for me."

Camden covered her mouth, coaxing her lips apart. She gripped the back of his neck and pulled him in even closer as she aligned their bodies from hip to chest. They always fit so flawlessly. How the hell were they not meant to be when everything seemed so right?

Okay, maybe not everything was perfect, but nothing in this world was. Delilah was *his* perfect.

Delilah pulled back and cocked her head with

a saucy grin. Damn it, that woman knew exactly what to do to get his blood pressure up in the very best way. She hooked her thumbs in the waistband of her little shorts and slid them down her shapely legs, then kicked them aside. She slowly pulled the crop tank up and over her head, also discarding it without a care.

"Make love to me," she commanded. "Out here, with the sunset in the background. I want to stay in this fantasy for as long as possible."

Camden rid himself of his clothes in record time and had the distance closed between them in one stride. He gripped Dee by her backside and lifted her against his body, then carried her over to one of the plush sectional sofas. He eased her down right in the corner and immediately dropped to his knees.

"I can never get enough of you," he told her. "You're it for me."

He slid his hands over the outside of her calves and on up to her knees, moving over her smooth skin to her inner thighs as he spread her farther apart. Delilah leaned back and inched down toward him, silently pleading for him to touch her. That familiar look in her eyes had his own arousal pumping. She could give him a look that would make him do anything she asked.

His thumbs grazed over her core and she gasped, tilting her hips. Looking up her body was his absolute favorite view, but having her here in this home he'd bought for them to work on rebuilding their future was a whole other level of much-needed bliss.

"Wait." Delilah moved back and edged around him to come to her feet.

"Stand up," she commanded. "I think you need to be properly thanked."

His entire body stirred as he came to his feet and kept his eyes on hers. She smiled and reached out, trailing her fingertips over his bare chest and farther down. Then she dropped to her knees, her mouth closing around him. Camden slid his fingers through her hair and groaned as she pleasured him with her mouth. He ground his teeth to keep some sort of control, but he had never been able to hold himself back with Delilah.

He selfishly enjoyed the moment, but then stepped back and lifted her up. He was about to lay her on the sofa when she pressed her hands flat against his chest and pushed him down. With a smile on her face, she straddled his lap and arched her back, silently offering up her breasts.

Another aspect he could never deny. She was absolute perfection, especially with the kiss of the sun on her skin.

Delilah joined their bodies as he cupped her breasts in his hands. She groaned as she rocked against him. Her hands rested on his shoulders and the slight sting into his skin from her fingertips had his body climbing higher. And from the way she was breathing and biting her bottom lip, she was damn close to her own release.

Camden gripped her face and pulled her mouth down to his. She opened freely for him as he swept his tongue into her mouth. She jerked her hips harder, faster, and let go.

Her entire body tightened around him, but he held her in place, not wanting to break that kiss until he had to. Camden's body tightened as he let himself go, too. Delilah shifted her lips over his and lightened the kiss as the tension from her body relaxed.

Once his own climax had waned, he nipped at her lips, feathering his mouth across hers.

"I think this balcony is my new favorite spot on the island," he told her.

Delilah stared down at him, her dark hair falling down around them. "I'm still partial to the cabana."

Camden slid his hands to her backside and carefully came to his feet. She wrapped her legs around his waist and rested her head on his shoulder.

"Where are we going?" she asked.

"I thought we could go lie in the bed and finish watching this sunset." He stepped into the bedroom and made his way to the bed. "Then we can go back out and I can see how your skin looks under a starry sky."

He laid her on the bed and his heart flipped when she stared up at him. Her midnight hair spread all around her on the stark white bedding. Her skin was still all flushed from the intimacy.

"I wouldn't mind seeing the stars with you," she told him with a wide smile. "We should rest, though. I might want to take a longer look at the stars than we did the sunset."

She was going to be the death of him. Her words…her actions. She knew exactly what to say and do to make him completely powerless where she was concerned.

He lay down next to her and wrapped his arms around her. A sense of peace settled over him. Right at this moment, nothing was wrong in his life. He chose to embrace this exact time with his wife in his arms, a gorgeous sunset in the distance, and the hope that something promising was coming from their time together.

Delilah stared out the window as the plane lifted from the runway. He knew she wasn't ready to say goodbye to this remote little island, but they both had treasured memories locked deep inside. No matter the outcome between them, nothing could erase the magic they'd shared over the past four days.

If four days with no outside interruptions could heal so much, what would happen if they tried this marriage again and focused more on each other and carving out that private time? While they hadn't broached those subjects, he had to believe they would, and because of what they'd experienced in the last few days, there was a new hope that once they had real talks, there might be a chance. He wanted to believe that, but he still had to be cautious.

Cam rested his hand on her thigh and Delilah turned to face him. From the look on her face, she definitely wasn't ready to leave. There was something so special about the memories that had taken place on this island—memories that would last a lifetime.

"We'll come back," he vowed.

"That implies there's a future for us."

He slid his thumb beneath her chin and tipped her head up slightly, then closed his lips over hers. The brief kiss only served one point and that was to show her, to make her feel, that he wanted to be with her and make this work.

"There can be a future for us," he told her.

She closed her eyes and dropped her forehead against his. He knew thoughts were racing through her head and he had no doubt she was already starting to think of all the obstacles in their way.

"These past few days make me want to believe that," she muttered. "There are just so many things, major things, that we didn't discuss before we married and we've glossed over since."

Camden had to do something to alleviate her worry, to prove to her that they could start taking steps toward the life she wanted...the life they both deserved.

"I know the timing of this topic might not be the best, but I need you to know something." He pulled back and took both of her hands between his as the plane leveled out. "If we stay together and decide to start our own family, I never want you to worry about where my loyalties would lie. I would love nothing more than to have a child with you, but mostly because I think we'd be kick-ass parents and we both have so much to offer."

"Children aren't really on my radar, especially right now," she replied. "I'm so busy with my job and with the animosity surrounding us from your parents, added with how busy you always stay with work...it wouldn't be fair to any child to bring them into this mess."

Camden nodded. "I agree with everything you said, that's why I need you to know—that chapter in our lives would be completely different. So if we have a family someday, fine. If we don't, that's fine, too. What matters is working on us."

Delilah eased her head down onto his shoulder and blew out a sigh. Silence filled the cabin and he wasn't about to push. This getaway had gone even better than he'd ever imagined, so he couldn't expect her to move right back in and pick up where they left off.

No. That's not where they needed to be. They had to start in a better spot than they left off.

Delilah didn't say anything else and after a while, he noticed her breathing had softened, her body had gone lax against his.

Carefully, so as to not wake her, Cam eased his arm around her back and cradled her against his side. He scooted slightly down, taking her with him so she wasn't so upright.

The fact she'd fallen asleep on him took him back to when they very briefly dated. He'd taken her to a concert and on the ride back home, he'd taken her hand and they'd sat in silence while he drove and she ultimately fell asleep. He didn't recall a time that she'd gotten that relaxed since.

Delilah was always go, go, go, and he thought that's what made them so perfect for each other. But now Cam was starting to see that she had been going nonstop with her work and start-up for Angel's Share all while trying to keep their marriage afloat. He'd been so damn oblivious, he'd thought everything was fine.

Well, other than his parents never approving and still trying to be part of his life but not Delilah's. After spending all of this time with her, his future was still quite questionable, but his goals had completely shifted. There was still so much left to explore in their relationship and giving up wasn't an option. He'd said that before, but his eyes and his mindset had been opened up and he had a clearer vision now.

Everything was at stake…and not just failing. There was so much more to this marriage than winning or losing. And the real possibility of having Dee walk out on him forever scared the hell out of him.

Camden closed his eyes and rested his head against the back of the couch as his own thoughts swirled around inside his head. He was already calculating what clients he could shift to his colleagues and what upcoming trips he could postpone or also hand off. He owned the damn firm. It's about time he acted like it and trusted his staff to handle more cases instead of overseeing every single thing.

As far as his parents, he was going to have to have yet another discussion with them. There was going to be an ultimatum declared and if they didn't like it, well…he'd have to deal with that when and if that happened.

Eleven

"Come back home."

Delilah stilled as Camden's bold command came out of nowhere. They'd landed safely and Camden had brought her luggage over and loaded it into the trunk of her car. She'd had every intention of talking about their future while on the plane, but she'd finally run out of energy.

Their precious, stolen time had come to an end and she was still so confused. Of course she wanted everything to be perfect and dreamlike the way it had been on their island. But she was realistic and that's just not how life worked.

Were they strong enough now? Was this reconciliation even a possibility?

"I'm not asking for an answer about our future,"

he added, reaching out to slide his hand into hers. "I'm asking you to give me another day because I'm not ready to spend another night without you."

Neither was she.

Delilah pulled in a deep breath and nodded. "I'll come over. Let me run back to my house first and change out my bag. I'll grab a few extra things and we'll see how one night goes."

Camden's smile widened. "Grabbing extra things sounds promising."

"I'm not promising anything yet."

He grazed his lips across hers. "But you didn't tell me goodbye."

Then he stepped back and moved his sunglasses from the top of his head to cover his eyes. "See you in a bit. At home."

At home.

This whole situation seemed too perfect, like they were moving fast again.

Just like they did the first time.

But Cam had said he wasn't looking for a solid, definite answer. No, he wanted one more night… and honestly, so did she.

Delilah got into her car and pulled out of the lot. She wasn't going to analyze this moment. She didn't have to be at work until tomorrow morning so she was going to enjoy the rest of her time off.

Then she'd have to go to her sisters and beg

them to help her figure out what the hell she was going to do.

Elise and Sara were probably the worst ones to ask, though. Elise was still in that happy stage where hearts were dancing all around her head and Sara was like a walking happily-ever-after movie. The woman believed in love and she believed there was one person for everyone.

Added to that, both of her sisters loved Camden and had tried to give her advice over the years. Now, though, she was more confused than ever.

Delilah made it to her rental and back to Camden's within an hour. She was surprised he didn't come out to greet her, but she grabbed her bag and her purse and headed up toward the front door.

She stood there for a half second trying to figure out if she should knock or just walk right in... which was ridiculous. This was still her house and if she wanted to start moving forward with Cam, she needed to show how she felt.

Dee opened the door and stepped into the two-story foyer. Old habits had her immediately turning to punch in the alarm code. She shifted back around and took in the place she'd called home for five years.

The ambience was exactly the same. The only thing that was different was the vase that used to be on the accent table by the door. That vase had been a gift from Milly for their wedding, but now it was secured in Bubble Wrap packed away in some box, probably still in the spare bedroom. For the past seven months she'd been meaning to get the rest of her things, but she'd gotten busy with work and one excuse after another had gotten in the way.

Delilah glanced toward the wide staircase leading toward the second floor and wondered if Camden was up there. A smile spread across her face as she sat her purse on top of her suitcase. Most likely he'd already started some sort of surprise for her, knowing him. She kept telling him she didn't like surprises, but he'd been so right in calling her out. She just didn't like that lack of control.

But he'd done a stellar job so far, so maybe she could learn to let go more.

Camden had been trying so hard to make her happy, which she appreciated. But at the same time, she didn't want him to feel like he had to do these things in order to keep her. Just being present was a huge improvement and she wished she could see into the future to see if he would keep that promise. She wished she could trust her gut and trust Cam to see his promises through.

Delilah started toward the staircase, but the light in the den down the hall caught her attention. She moved toward the room where Camden usually did late-night work. Odd that he would be in there now when he knew she was coming over.

As she stepped into the doorway, there he was

standing at his desk, holding several papers in his hands. He still had on his shorts and T-shirt from this afternoon when they'd left the island. Clearly, whatever he was staring at was troublesome since he hadn't even noticed she was here.

Worry niggled at her and she could practically feel the invisible walls of reality closing in on them once again.

"Is everything okay?" she asked, remaining in the doorway.

He jerked his head up. "Dee. I didn't hear you come in."

Obviously. Concerned, she stepped into the room and stopped at the leather sofa. She eased her hip onto the arm and tried to see what he was holding, but he wasn't offering any insight. She tried to remain calm, but this wasn't the same Cam who she'd spent the last four days with and this wasn't the same man she'd just left at the airport who had asked her to stay.

"You seem a million miles away."

"They came," he said, holding up the documents for her to see.

He didn't have to tell her what "they" were. Her heart clenched; her breath caught in her throat.

The divorce papers. The first set had been wrong and had to be completely redone and now they were back. All she and Cam had to do was sign.

If this wasn't a slap of reality to the face after such a beautiful getaway…

Delilah clasped her hands in her lap and chewed on the inside of her cheek. She wasn't even sure what to say, what to do, and clearly Cam was in the same boat considering the room was dead silent.

It was that silence that spoke volumes. They were at a fork in the road and neither of them wanted to take the next step for fear of making the wrong decision.

"I… I wasn't expecting to come home to this," he finally stated. "I was just hoping for junk mail."

He turned and tossed the papers onto his desk before shifting his attention back to her. Cam rested his hands on his narrow hips and met her gaze, clearly waiting on something from her. She'd never seen him look defeated, but if there was ever a time, this would be it. His shoulders weren't so square now, his jawline lax, and his dark eyes were shielded by heavy lids. A punch of guilt and remorse hit her. She never wanted anyone to go through pain, not her or him. But she also had to think of long-term ramifications, and if staying would only hurt them more in the long run…

At this point, she wasn't so sure.

"I'm not sure what to do here," she told him. "I mean, a week ago I would have been ready to sign just to have a clean cut and move on. I would have signed to set us both free of this heartache."

He remained in place, as did his intense gaze. "And now?"

"That's the proverbial elephant in the room, isn't it?" She came to her feet, unable to sit still any longer. "If we sign, that's it. Our marriage is over. If we don't, then we're both saying there's a chance for something more, a fresh start."

She paced across the room to the desk and stared down at the papers. Their names in bold print stared back up, but it was the photo on the desk that caught her attention. It was a photo she'd seen there so many times and never thought much about it...until now.

She and Cam were kissing under a waterfall on their honeymoon in Kauai. That day had been amazing. They'd hiked for hours and then found the waterfall and dived right into the refreshing water. They'd been on a tour and hadn't known the guide had taken the picture until they were ready to check out of their resort.

Once they'd gotten home, Delilah had put the picture in a frame and Cam had immediately claimed it as his own. There were times she forgot about the photo until she had a reason to come in here, but for the past five years, that photo had been there where he wanted it, maybe where he needed it to be. Perhaps he looked at it and remembered the best time of their lives. While she didn't have the image to look at all the time, she did have the memories that she often pulled back up on rough days.

Delilah's eyes went from the photo to the papers and back to the photo. So much had happened from one event to the next.

"Say something."

Delilah turned her attention to Camden, who stood with his hands still on his hips, looking just as frustrated as she felt. But he kept his gaze locked on her. And, honestly, she wasn't sure if he was frustrated or terrified of what would come out of her mouth.

The chime from the front doorbell echoed through the foyer and down the hallway. When he didn't make a move, Delilah came around the desk.

"Are you expecting someone?" she asked.

"No, and nothing is more important than this."

She started to pass him, but he slid his arm around her waist before she could.

"Ignore it," he said.

His concentrated look left her no choice but to remain still. They did need to talk about the future, whether together or separate. While the getaway had been perfect, they were back to reality and all that came with it. Decisions would have to be made. She just didn't think she'd have this much trouble.

But when love was the center of everything, that made leaving so damn hard. If she didn't love him so much, this would've been an easy break. But perhaps their love had been misplaced. Maybe they loved the idea of the marriage, of being a dynamic team. Love had to flow between them, building a bridge that would keep them forged together forever.

The doorbell chimed once again and Camden jerked away, muttering a curse as he headed out of the room. Delilah blew out a sigh at the intensity of the moment and she didn't know if she cursed the unwanted guest or wanted to thank them for giving her a moment to think.

Moments later, Dee heard familiar voices and she stepped out into the hallway. Nothing good was going to come from this because if she thought the last few minutes had been trying, the next few were going to put that to the test.

Cam stood in the entryway with his parents and all eyes turned to her. Great, just what she needed to top off seeing her divorce papers…one of the main reminders of why they were in this situation to begin with.

Twelve

Camden wished more than anything he had not answered the door.

No, he wished he and Delilah had stayed on their own private island and said to hell with the rest of the world.

"We've been calling and texting for days," his mother fussed. "We were worried sick, Camden. We've been coming by, but then we saw her car and knew you were here."

Camden glanced over his shoulder as Delilah started down the hallway toward them. He wanted to shield her from any hurtful words that were no doubt about to be said, but he also knew she had her pride and wanted to stand on her own. There was such a fine line here.

"I forgot to give his phone back," Dee stated as she moved toward her bag in the foyer. "It's been off for a few days."

His mother rolled her eyes. "Of course you've had it. No wonder I couldn't get hold of my son."

"I texted you both and said I'd be out of town," Cam told them. "Is there an emergency?"

His mother's eyes went to Delilah, then back to Camden. "Not an emergency, but if you had listened to your messages or had she given them to you, you would know we are planning a trip to Tahoe. We actually wondered if you'd like to join us and get away to decompress. You've been dealing with so much."

Camden raked a hand over the back of his neck trying to ease the tension.

"We actually just got back from a trip, so I'll pass."

Both of his parents glanced at Delilah, who had come to stand beside him now. She handed over his phone and he pocketed it.

"So she's controlling you now?" his mother asked. "Money wasn't enough for her?"

"Listen—"

"I don't want, nor have I ever needed Cam's money," Delilah stated, cutting him off. "I don't know why you always say that or imply that I cannot take care of myself. I am part owner in a lucrative business and this marriage was never based on anything other than love. And I'm tired of defending myself to you. I'm tired of the way you're always meddling and making Camden feel like he's being torn in two and has to decide between his parents and his wife. You should be ashamed of yourselves."

Camden had to bite the inside of his cheek to keep from smiling. He also had to keep his applause inside his head, too. Delilah had never talked to his parents in such a way. In all honesty, she typically avoided them since they'd let it be known from the start that they didn't approve of her middle-class upbringing.

Damn, she delivered a verbal punch that had been a long time coming. Yes, they were his parents and he loved them, but Dee had put up with more than enough over the years.

"Nobody talks to me that way," his mother sneered.

Delilah reached down and grabbed her bag and purse. "I just did."

Camden gripped her elbow. "Don't go."

"You three need to talk without me and I need to get back to reality. Unfortunately, this is it."

Camden watched as she walked out of his house—their house. How the hell had he gone from bliss this afternoon to heartache tonight?

Dee was right. This was their reality for right now and something had to change. He had to change.

"I cannot believe you went on a trip with her."

His mother crossed her arms over her chest. "What happened to the divorce?"

"What Delilah and I are doing or not doing is none of your concern," Camden informed her. "I've let this go on for far too long, thinking you two would come around to seeing what an amazing woman she is."

"Son, we just don't think she's the one for you," his father stated in that softer tone of his that grated on Cam's nerves.

"It doesn't matter what the two of you think because I'm the one married to her."

"For now," his mother quickly added.

No. That wasn't right at all. None of this was ever meant to be temporary and the marriage never should have been about winning or losing. He loved Delilah, more than he'd ever admitted—maybe even to himself. He needed her, more than he needed to succeed.

"Forever, if she'll stay," Cam chimed in. "Though I can't blame her for wanting out. She says it's to set me free, but the truth is, she's been stuck here trying to hold a marriage together that you two condemned every chance you got. But I have to take some of the blame as well. My work schedule is too much and I didn't realize that."

"She's trying to control you," his mother fired back. "You are too successful to back down."

"I'll still be just as successful, but I'd at least have a happy marriage. I hope."

Cam waited for one of them to say something else. The tension in the foyer had gotten out of control. He wanted Delilah back here; he wanted to carry on with the night they had planned. He wondered what she was thinking now. Was her mind on those damn papers in his den? Was she wishing she'd never come here tonight?

He hoped like hell she realized he had her back. He would always have her back, from here on out, no matter what.

So in a sense, he was deciding between his wife and his parents and he didn't know why it took him so long to realize.

"You both have put me in a position that I feel like I do have to choose one family or the other."

His mother blinked and jerked as if he'd slapped her.

"She is the one making you choose," she defended. "Not us."

"Actually, she's the one who walked away to try to save my relationship with you two." His heart ached just thinking about what she'd sacrificed. "So don't throw down your noble card just yet."

"Camden—"

"No." Cam held up his hand, cutting off his father. "I'm working on my marriage. You guys can either support that or not, that will be your decision. But know that if you force my hand in choosing, you won't like the outcome."

His mother's gasp echoed in the foyer. Frustration and fatigue hit Cam and he just wanted to be done here. He'd said what he needed to say and all he cared about at this moment was Delilah. She'd been through too much and he'd let it go, hoping everyone would eventually come around.

No matter his parents' initial thoughts on Dee, couldn't they see that she was a genuine person? That she loved and was loyal and stood on her own? If anything, he needed her. Not the other way around.

Camden stepped around his parents and went to the door. He opened it and turned to them.

"We're done here," he told them. "Enjoy your trip to Tahoe."

The silence and intensity went on for longer than he was comfortable with, but they ultimately left and Cam closed the door, reset the alarm system and raked a hand down his face. This whole day had done a complete one-eighty and he had no clue what to do next.

Did Delilah want space? Did she want him to come to her?

How the hell could he be so in control of his firm, his career, and lose hold of his family? His priorities were shifting and part of him worried what would happen if he eased up on work. His entire life he'd been molded to be a successful attorney, working for the next promotion, the next milestone. Once he'd gotten his own firm and started employing the best lawyers, he'd grown to that next level. His name was well-known among the most elite clientele.

No doubt he'd made his parents proud, which was what he'd wanted when he'd been younger. As an only child, who wouldn't want the accolades?

But then he'd met Delilah and suddenly he wasn't their perfect son doing everything they wished. Slowly, so damn slowly, he'd started seeing that he'd been like clay to his parents. They'd shaped him into precisely the man they'd wanted him to become. Prestigious and wealthy.

Had he lost himself along the way? Is that why finding and marrying Delilah had been so appealing? She'd breathed new life into his world…she still did. He was going to fight for her, for them, to prove to her that she did come in first place in his life from here on out.

Cam wasn't sure if Delilah needed the space tonight or not, but he was going to give it to her because he needed to clear his own head. There were going to be some major changes coming up and he wasn't sure how everything would turn out. He could be putting everything on the line for a marriage that was still doomed to failure, but he wasn't going to just let the best thing in his life slip away.

Now, more than ever, he was determined to make this right.

* * *

"You look like hell."

Delilah glanced up from her computer and spotted Elise in the doorway to her office. She sank back in her leather chair and sighed.

"You're always so forthcoming with those sweet compliments," Delilah replied.

"I mean that in the best way." Elise stepped into the room and closed the door behind her. "It's my way of asking what's wrong? Because I thought I'd come in this morning and you'd be all chipper and ready to go after taking a sabbatical."

Yeah, well, she probably would have been if she hadn't been up all night worrying, pacing, playing out every scenario in her head of different paths in her life…wondering why Cam hadn't texted, called or come by.

What had happened between him and his parents when she left? Did anything get resolved? Did he tell them they were working on the marriage? Did they try to talk him out of moving forward with her? No doubt they reminded him over and over of how successful he was and how career and finances came above all else. Delilah doubted those two even knew what love was and she highly doubted they even loved each other.

"Where did you go, anyway?"

"To Georgia with Cam."

There was no reason to lie or evade the question. Her sisters were her very best friends, and now more than ever, she needed them. She really wished she had Milly for some sound advice, but Elise and Sara would be just as solid. They were all raised by the same astounding woman, and Delilah knew she'd get through this.

Silence settled between them as Elise sat with eyes wide open. Finally, she pulled out her cell, her fingers rushing over the screen.

"What—"

"Don't say anything else," Elise commanded. "Sara is on her way. We need details."

"We have jobs to do," Delilah reminded her.

"Tours are covered, every employee showed up today, no meetings or VIP clients are scheduled. We have the time."

Of course they'd make her rehash this right now. Delilah had hoped she'd come into work and get caught up before getting into everything. But better to just get it over with.

Sara burst into the office, immediately blowing her hair out of her face and closing the door behind her.

"I ran up here and I just know that tour starting thought I had a raging case of diarrhea."

Delilah couldn't help but laugh. "I'm sure they didn't think that."

"You spent the last four days with Camden?"

Sara asked, taking a seat next to Elise across from Dee's desk.

"I'm laying it all out now and I'll take questions at the end," she informed them. "Cam asked me to give him four days to work on our marriage. So I met him at the airport, and we flew to a private island off the Georgia coast, which I found out he bought for us, by the way. The house was amazing and secluded with our own beach and cabana. We flew home, our new divorce papers had arrived and then his parents showed up and wasted no time in declaring their disdain for me once again. That pretty much sums up my last four days. Questions?"

Her statement was met with shocked stares and silence. There had been quite the whirlwind of emotions and events that Delilah was still trying to process herself, so no doubt her sisters were rolling over everything she'd just dropped on them.

"Does this mean you guys are getting back together?" Sara finally asked.

"That's the million-dollar question," Delilah replied. "We know what we want, but at the same time, I have to be realistic. I don't know what happened after I left last night. Cam and his parents likely had a heated discussion."

"Are they so stuck in their high-society ways that they still can't let you in?" Elise asked in disbelief. "I mean, they do see that we have a very successful business, right?"

"It's my background, I'm sure," Dee explained. "We all had humble beginnings, no real parents, and Milly was a simple schoolteacher. Nothing too exciting or bragworthy in their world."

Elise rolled her eyes. "Those two aren't anything to brag about, either. I don't care what job or rank someone has. Treating people equally and respectfully is more important than anything."

Delilah nodded in agreement. "They didn't get that memo in grammar school."

"Have you talked to Camden since last night?" Sara asked.

"I haven't. No text or anything. I'm sure he's overwhelmed. That's just one of the reasons I'm trying to set him free."

"Oh, would you just stop with that nonsense?" Elise scolded. "Marriage takes two people and it's so obvious you two love each other."

"Love isn't the only thing that keeps people together," Delilah replied.

"No, you're right, but Antonio and I overcame obstacles and we're going to make it work." Elise leaned forward in her seat and held Dee's gaze. "Listen, I'm not judging you or saying you guys didn't work, but I think you both were working at the wrong things. Now that you know what the enemy is, you can better tackle it."

Delilah sighed. "There's just so much, and I know I definitely take part blame for not speaking up and standing up before now, but I just thought things would get better, you know? But his work always comes first, his parents are against us, and what about if we ever start a family? I don't even know if that's something I'm ready for. Is that terrible?"

"Just because you're married doesn't mean you have to have children," Sara told her. "There's no rule book as to what you have to do with your life. What you and Cam need to do is get back to why you fell in love to begin with, before all this other stuff got in your way."

"That's why he wanted us to have that getaway," Delilah murmured. "He just wanted us without all the outside noise."

"Can we focus on the fact he bought you an island?" Sara laughed. "Because that is the most romantic thing I've ever heard."

Delilah couldn't help but smile. "It was pretty damn cool," she agreed. "He bought it before I asked for the divorce. He was going to surprise me. But once I left, he said he had the house remodeled to mimic various parts of our honeymoon."

"Okay, now *that* is the most romantic thing I've ever heard," Sara corrected.

"The house and island were pretty remarkable."

Too remarkable. Too perfect. And he'd done

all of that for her not even knowing if she'd ever be there. He had that hope, so surely she could, too. Right?

"So what are you going to do?" Elise asked.

Delilah sat forward in her seat and rested her arms on her desk. She'd analyzed this situation from every single angle and still didn't have a solid answer.

"My biggest fear is that I go back and we end up here in six months or a year. If nothing changes, I've gotten my hopes up again and I'm in for even more heartache."

"But what if you go back and everything is absolutely beautiful?" Sara asked.

Delilah's cell vibrated on her desk and she glanced down to see Cam's name. She tapped the screen to pull up his message.

We need to talk

Yes, they did, but what would this conversation be about?

"What is it?" Sara asked.

Delilah glanced at her sisters. "Cam wants to talk."

"Then go," Elise stated, waving her hands. "Get out of here and go talk."

Delilah shook her head. "No. I'm working today

and so is he. I'll tell him we can meet up tonight. I still need to think a little more before I see him."

When her sisters just continued to stare, Delilah tipped her head and smiled.

"I'll figure this out, so stop looking so worried."

"We can't help it," Sara told her. "But since you're thinking on Cam and we're up to speed, can I ask an opinion?"

"Of course." Delilah was so ready to change topics. "What's up?"

Sara pulled her cell from her pocket and typed in a few things before turning it around. "This is some information I found out about my father. I think his name was James, but I don't know anything else."

"Oh my word, Sara," Elise exclaimed. "You have a name. That's incredible. Your investigator works fast."

"I paid her enough to do so," Sara replied, then turned her cell back and scrolled more. "It might be a long shot, but my investigator said the timing is right for a guy named James who actually worked as a counselor at one of the facilities supposedly our mother had worked on during one time when she was clean."

Delilah was pretty impressed with the fact they had a name for Sara's father. Even though they all had different fathers, they were in this situation together and had to support each other no matter their decisions.

"What if she finds out more?" Sara asked. "I mean, what if I get his information and he's alive? What if he still lives around here? Does he know I exist?"

"Those are all the same questions we've asked ourselves," Elise replied. "I'm still fine with not knowing. I love Antonio and the life we're going to have together. I just want to look forward to that. But I'm here for both of you, no matter what you decide."

"Agreed," Delilah said with a nod. "I want to, but it's just all the rest of the chaos in my life that's not letting me focus on my biological father."

Elise came to her feet and glanced down at Delilah. She offered that soft smile that often-times looked like Sara's…that trait had to have been from their mother.

"Tackle one major life issue at a time," Elise stated. "And whenever you all are ready, we'll get rolling on this wedding of mine."

Sara clasped her hands. "Girl, I got you. I've condensed the spreadsheet just for you."

Delilah snorted. "I'm ready whenever you are. It will be refreshing to focus on something solid and positive. Besides, working today on packages for events and weddings is the top of my list… ironically so."

Elise wrinkled her nose. "Do you want me to take that over?"

"Absolutely not." Delilah stood and shook her

head. "I love my job and I want to do something creative. So, this and your wedding planning will be perfect."

Sara also stood and slid her cell back into the pocket of her maxi dress. "If anything gets overwhelming, for either of you, come to me. I've got no social life right now, so I'm available. Just living with the anxiety over what my investigator will find out."

Delilah came around her desk and opened her arms. "Bring it in, girls. We haven't done a group hug forever and I think we all need one."

Her sisters gathered in and their foreheads touched as they huddled together. This might do more for Delilah's spirits than anything else. No matter what, she knew these women would have her back. They'd support her and comfort her no matter what and she'd do the same for them.

"Do we have to go back to work?" Sara asked. "I'm interviewing for a new gift shop manager. I hate doing interviews. I think I get more nervous than the applicants."

"I'll do it," Elise said. "It gives me a break from sales reports."

Delilah shifted in her chair and clasped her hands together. "That's settled then. You two get back to work and let me get caught up. We'll talk later."

"You'll let us know if there's any developments

with Camden?" Elise asked as she headed toward the door.

"Of course, but you guys don't have to run up here if I text. Just go about business as usual."

Sara snorted. "Nothing about our lives right now is business as usual. We're all up in the air in one manner or another and Milly's house is still not—"

"Don't do it," Elise groaned. "Don't say there's more to clean out. I can't handle anything else right now. That house isn't going anywhere, but my sanity is."

"Fine." Sara crossed to the door and stood by Elise. "We'll wait to discuss, but you better keep us updated about Cam."

Delilah nodded and waited until her sisters were out of her office before she reached for her phone on her desk and fired back a text.

Meet me at my house after work

She didn't want to go back to the house they shared. If they wanted to talk and be alone, her new place was best. His parents didn't even know where that house was, so they wouldn't be interrupted.

Delilah had no clue where they stood, but talking about those papers and his parents had to come above all else. Definitely not the alone time she wanted with her husband.

Thirteen

Camden didn't want to go to her rental. That's not how he wanted to progress in their journey to reunite. He wanted to bring her home, where she belonged.

When she'd texted and told him to meet at her place, he'd waited a bit and mulled it over. Talking things over at her rental didn't sit well with him and it really shouldn't to her, either. He thought he'd get some backlash from her when he texted back saying he preferred their house. After several long minutes she'd agreed to meet him at his house. She kept referring to it as his, but he wasn't going to have any part of that.

They shared this place. Her stamp was all over it, from the wall art she'd chosen to hang in their bedroom, to the flowers she'd planted herself around their porch, to the sofa she'd fallen in love with and ordered even though he'd told her it was hideous. Every room had memories of Delilah, but he wanted the real deal.

He'd just poured her a glass of wine when the front door alarm echoed through the foyer. Camden sat the glass on the wet bar and moved through the living room to greet her. As he stepped through the wide arched doorway to the foyer, Delilah turned after resetting the alarm. She smoothed the moisture from the rain away from her face and sat her purse on the accent table. She didn't have a bag, which meant she hadn't planned on staying. That silent act spoke volumes for how this night would go.

"Hey," she greeted with a smile.

She'd left her dark hair down around her shoulders and had changed from her office clothes. Her black leggings hugged her long legs and she'd put on an oversize tee that hung off one slender shoulder. He didn't care if she dressed up or dressed down—or didn't dress at all—she was still the most remarkable woman he'd ever known.

Water droplets clung to her silky hair and her face glistened with dampness. With her dark skin and hair and that shoulder playing peekaboo, she looked like a seductress.

But there was something vulnerable beneath

that sultry exterior. She looked terrified or worried or perhaps both. The last time they'd stood here had been so intense that he still hadn't recovered, and he had no idea where she was in her headspace.

"I have a glass of pinot in here for you," he offered, gesturing to the living room.

A smile spread across her face as her shoulders softened. "That sounds perfect. I've barely been able to catch my breath after work today."

"It's always a bit overwhelming that first day back after taking time off," he agreed.

Delilah took a seat on the chaise portion of the sofa while Camden went to get her drink. When he turned back around, she'd toed her shoes off and had already propped her feet up. The way she stared back at him already had his desires stirring, but they seriously had to talk.

He handed her the wine and stood over her, resting his hands on his hips.

"Are you hungry? I can go find you something."

Delilah took a sip and then shook her head. "No. Elise brought me a late lunch."

"You're not staying the night."

He didn't ask, but he wanted that put out there. He wanted to dive right into this conversation and work through any confusion or misconception. Because he'd assumed she'd want to spend the night…he'd hoped she did.

"I'm not," she agreed, licking the wine from

her lips. "We need to talk and sometimes sex gets in the way of us staying on track and focusing."

Oh, he was damn well focused on his wife. He'd been unable to focus on anything else.

"Just because you're not spending the night, doesn't mean we won't have sex," he countered.

A hint of a smile danced around her lips. "True, but I'm trying to avoid temptation as much as possible."

"You're saying I'm too tempting?"

She shrugged and took another sip without answering.

Camden eased down to the foot of the chaise, next to her legs. He rested his hand on her thigh and stared back into her dark gaze. He'd gone over and over what he would say to her once they were alone again, but words failed him. He wasn't going to beg—he'd never be that person. Delilah either wanted to stay or she didn't.

His purpose was to show her exactly why she should. This marriage was worth fighting for.

"I want you to stay," he told her.

"I'm aware." She swirled the contents of her glass and glanced down. "There's just so much to process and I don't know what happened with your parents after I left. I never heard anything."

She brought her attention back to him, clearly waiting on a reply.

"I gave them the ultimatum that should have

been done before now," he explained. "If I have to choose between two families, then that's what I'll have to do. It sucks, it's unfair to everyone, but I won't keep putting you through this."

"And that's exactly what I didn't want to happen. I don't want to be the reason you guys have a falling-out that you might never recover from."

He squeezed her leg. "You aren't the reason for their narrow minds."

"No, but I am the reason for the rift."

Camden took her glass of wine and sat it on the side table. Turning back, he rested his hands on either side of her hips and closed in.

"I won't live like this anymore," he told her. "We won't live like this."

"I want to believe it," she whispered, her eyes darting to her lap. "I want to think you and I will always put each other first."

Her expressive midnight gaze slid back up just as a crack of thunder shook the windows. Of course a storm surrounded them…that seemed to be the theme as of late.

"What happens when you slide back into working and traveling so much? Maybe I'm selfish and maybe I'm a hypocrite for wanting you to spend more time with me when I work so much, too."

Cam nodded in agreement. "Trying to get a new business off the ground requires work. We both had a tendency to assume the other would just be there."

Delilah reached her hand up and slid her palm over his jawline. Cam reached up and covered her hand with his own.

"When you left, nothing else mattered," he admitted. "Nothing. I had to drag myself into work to keep occupied and make sure my clients' needs were met, but all of my thoughts were on you and us and how the hell I let things get so out of control."

Delilah closed her eyes and sighed. "I'm tired. So tired of thinking this is a failure, tired of not being able to hold on to what I want and tired of the fear that if I open my heart wide again and it gets broken, I'll never be able to recover."

Hearing her so vulnerable and honest had his own heart cracking. He slid their joined hands down to her lap and held tight. Her lids fluttered open and there was no hiding her emotions. She looked at him as if seeking an answer she'd been needing— as if wanting him to tell her that their lives would be fine and she had nothing to worry about.

As much as he wanted his wife back, he also couldn't lie to her.

"I can't guarantee things will be perfect," he admitted. "All I can say is my priorities have shifted and I realize what is important."

"I swear, I never want to be that clingy, needy wife," she explained. "I just want to be a vital part of your life. I would never want you to feel like I love my job or anything else above you."

"The fact that you married me after knowing me such a short time speaks volumes," he told her with a smile. "You think about everything. You have all these detailed plans and are determined to check off every box. Once I realized that about you, I was shocked you agreed to marry me after only a few months of dating."

Delilah laughed. "I surprised myself, too, not to mention Milly and my sisters. They thought I was joking."

Camden shifted between her legs, maneuvering so he sat on the chaise and she straddled his lap. This was definitely one area of his life he didn't mind relinquishing control. He pulled her in tighter until she hovered just above him and her hair curtained their faces.

"We have something that has lasted five years," he explained. "Maybe they weren't the best five years, but I'm not ready to just give up and I won't let you, either. If I thought you truly wanted out, I'd step away, but I know you don't."

She rested her forehead against his. "No, I don't. I only wanted out to save both of us any more heartache."

Camden slid his hands down her back and to the hem of her shirt. Gathering the material in his hands, he eased back to keep all of his focus on her.

"You don't have to do anything anymore," he assured her. "You've fought for this marriage long enough and now I'm taking over."

He pulled the shirt up and over her head, tossing it aside. The lightning flashed once more as the thunder continued to boom.

"From here on out, I've got you," he vowed.

She opened her mouth to say something, but he wasn't in the mood to talk. That's why she'd come here, but seeing her again after that ordeal with his parents and knowing just how much she had sacrificed over the years only made her that much more precious to him.

His Delilah had stepped away so that he could repair a damaged relationship, but living without her wasn't an option. No matter what he had to do, he'd find a way to push on, even if he had to carry her the entire way.

Delilah's hands were up his shirt, her fingertips trailing along his bare skin. She started tugging and he pulled away just enough to rid himself of the tee. Then she came alive in his arms. Still straddling his lap, her hands went to work on his pants.

In a flurry of motions, they stood and completely stripped down to absolutely nothing. Camden went to the wall and dimmed the lights. He wanted nothing but that raging storm for the setting. The flashes of lightning lit up Delilah's bare skin as she lay back on the chaise and reached for him.

Damn it. This is where she belonged. There wasn't a doubt that she knew that.

She lifted her knees and eased her legs apart, silently pleading for him. He wasted no time in settling in right where they both wanted him to be. Flattening his hands on either side of her head, Camden leaned down to nip at her lips. His chest brushed against hers just as a groan escaped her. He reached down between them, feathering his fingertips over her core.

"Don't make me wait," she pleaded against his mouth.

Camden slid into her. He'd thought he would take things slow, but damn it, he couldn't. This moment didn't call for sweet and tender, but intense and powerful.

Delilah moved perfectly against him in a rhythm that matched his own. Clearly she was in a hurry as well. The lightning flashes came closer together as the rain pelted against the windows. Camden gripped the back of the sofa for leverage as he grew closer to his climax. Delilah cried out, wrapping her arms and legs tight around his body as she clung to him during her release.

Cam let go and followed, shutting his eyes as if he could lock this moment in time. He never wanted her to leave, didn't want their intimate moments to end.

But once his body calmed and Dee had gone

lax beneath him, he shifted to lie at her side. He still had one leg thrown over hers as he trailed his fingertips up and down her heated torso. Her body trembled beneath his touch and he hoped like hell she never got tired of him wanting her.

"I know I asked you to stay tonight, but I want you to stay forever."

She didn't reply. Silence filled the room while the storm continued its wrath outside. He wished she'd tell him what she was thinking, but maybe that was too much for her right now. He'd learned over the past seven months that she needed space. Hell, maybe they both did, because having her gone only proved to him how much he needed her and wanted her by his side.

Delilah reached up and stroked his beard. She sometimes did that before she fell asleep and it was a habit he'd missed. He cradled her tighter, knowing full well he'd slay any demons that threatened her happiness…even if that included his family.

"I was thinking about having the ceremony here."

Elise spread her arms wide at the outdoor garden area separating the main part of the castle and the old stone buildings they had turned into the rick houses that held all of their aging barrels.

The white blooms and all the lush greenery combined with the stone paths would be a gorgeous setting for an outdoor wedding.

"Is that okay with you?" Elise turned to Antonio, who was glancing around the open space.

"If this is what you want," he replied. "Do you have a backup area in case of bad weather?"

Elise smiled up at him and Delilah glanced at Sara, who was jotting down notes in her planner. Antonio and Elise had finally decided to get married in just a few weeks. The wedding planning would be rushed, but the couple wanted to be wed and at the end of the day, that's all that mattered.

Delilah made her own notes in her phone to remember to add various details and suggestions to the packages she was working on.

"I think the entryway into the castle would be perfect for any weddings held indoors," Sara chimed in without looking up from her notepad. "Especially if we go all dramatic and leave the drawbridge down."

"Yes, especially with all of those windows along the back wall," Delilah added. "It would be breathtaking and different."

Elise nodded. "I love it."

"We can also give other brides the option of using the ballroom," Delilah said, thinking out loud. "If they have the reception there, it's certainly big enough that we could use the stage at the front for the ceremony, set up chairs on the floor and run the aisle runner, but then keep all of the reception tables toward the back. There would still be room for the dance floor if the couple chooses that, too."

"Brilliant." Sara beamed. "This is going to take us next level. We are going to be booked solid once your photos get out and after the governor's daughter has her wedding here."

"I'm not sure I want a big wedding," Elise said, then turned to Antonio. "We discussed we really just want family and something intimate."

"That's even better," Sara stated. "We can advertise that no matter the size of your wedding party or guest list, we can accommodate."

"Do you want to have any draped tents with chandeliers, or what's the feel you two are going for?" Delilah asked.

"I'm just here to choose the spirits for the reception," Antonio said, laughing. "Elise can do anything she wants."

Elise pursed her lips and surveyed the area once again. "I think just open. I don't want to block any beautiful views, and we'll be going in for the reception. I really want to embrace the beauty of this property. I think once we start adding more elements out here, it takes away from the grounds and wouldn't seem as intimate."

"I agree with that," Antonio stated, then pulled his cell from his pocket and stared at the screen for a second. "Excuse me. I need to take this."

As he stepped away to answer his call, Elise's smile widened as she clasped her hands.

"This is really happening," she exclaimed. "I never thought I'd get married, let alone in a gorgeous place like this. Can you guys believe this?"

"Oh, I believe it." Dee laughed. "You two are perfect for each other and this is going to be a stunning wedding."

"I think so, too. His parents will be flying in from Spain the week before to help with anything we need." Elise slid her hands into the pockets of her dress pants and sighed. "They are seriously the nicest people and I can't wait to get to know them more. I mean, they raised an amazing man, so I feel I lucked out with this family."

"I can attest to that," Delilah said, nodding. "See what you're marrying into. It's going to be key in the long run."

Sara tipped her head and opened her mouth, but Elise stepped forward and put a hand on Delilah's arm.

"Are you sure this isn't too much?" she asked.

Delilah shook her head. "I promise, it's fine. I'm so happy for you guys and thrilled to be part of something so special."

Sara took a step forward. "Can I ask how things are with you and Cam? We haven't heard anything since yesterday in your office."

"I spent the night at the house," she confessed. "I hadn't planned on it. I went there to talk, but then…"

"Good for you guys," Elise cheered. "I know you think physical isn't everything, and it's not, but it also helps that connection and bond stay strong. So, what about those divorce papers?"

"That subject wasn't even brought up. I had to wake early to get back to my place and get ready."

Elise dropped her hand and crossed her arms. "Honey, why don't you just move your things back in?"

Delilah bit her lip and shrugged. "I'm thinking about it. He asked me if I'd stay tonight and I thought about showing up with a couple of bags. The only way to really try this again, to move forward, is to jump back in. But I'm terrified."

"Okay, what did I miss?"

Antonio came back and stood next to Elise, but glanced at all the sisters, then took a step back.

"Maldito."

Delilah had noticed when Antonio cursed, he always did so in Spanish. He had a thick accent, but they were all actually learning quite a bit from him, which Delilah loved. Broadening her scope of understanding other cultures would only be beneficial and respectful as their business continued to grow.

"Apparently we've moved on from the wedding," he stated. "I have more calls to make if you need more privacy."

Elise reached back and patted his arm. "That would be great. Why don't we meet you in the ballroom in a few minutes?"

Antonio leaned down and kissed Elise's cheek before he walked away.

"The way he looks at you is pretty intense," Dee told her sister.

Sara snorted. "Cam looks at you the exact same way."

Did he? She had no idea, but looking in from the outside was completely different than being in the situation. Camden had never made his feelings for her a secret, which was just one of the other reasons she loved him.

Maybe it was planning this wedding or perhaps it was the fact they had rekindled on a whole new level, but Delilah had high hopes for their future.

Fourteen

Delilah parked her car in front of the garage. Just pulling into her old spot had her smiling. Maybe coming home could be this easy. Maybe she'd been making this more difficult than it needed to be. If she and Cam could get on, and stay on, the same page, they could tackle anything together...she hoped.

It was that faith that had her back with two suitcases. She would stay through the weekend and see how they adjusted back to married life. Staying last night had opened her eyes to how much she had missed since moving out. Being in her own place had been lonely and odd. She'd only been renting because she wasn't sure where to go, so none of the things in the house were really hers.

She had a few personal belongings, but for the most part, she'd left furniture and major items for Camden.

When she'd left, she was certain she had to start fresh, make a clean break...but that was just naive thinking. There was no easy way out or a quick path to heal heartache and erase five years.

She never wanted to erase them. She wanted to use that time and learn from it so they could move forward and have the marriage they deserved.

Delilah popped the trunk of her car and went to get her luggage. She was a little surprised that Cam's car wasn't in the garage, but he should be home anytime. He'd be so surprised when he saw her bringing some things. Maybe she should hang some of her clothes back in her walk-in closet and add a few toiletries to her vanity in the en suite.

He would be so happy she was here and, honestly, she was quite giddy herself. The whole idea of them starting fresh and really holding on to those important aspects of this marriage is what would make them successful. Neither of them wanted to be a failure at anything. And some marriages weren't meant to last—that didn't make them failures. But Delilah knew this marriage was meant to be and if she left now, that would be failing. She and Camden could be stronger than ever now that they had the weapons to fight the negativity that had plagued them for years. They had a knowledge they'd never had before.

Delilah hoisted her luggage up the steps and then wheeled the bags into the bedroom. She wasted no time in unpacking and placing her things just like she used to have them. When she took a step back from her vanity and glanced into the mirror, she knew this was right. This *felt* right.

But her appearance was all wrong. If she was going to be back and ready for this new beginning, she had to look like she hadn't spent all day at work charming their VIP clients, as well as figuring out her newly created position of events coordinator.

Delilah glanced at the time and wondered where Camden was. He hadn't texted to tell her he'd be late or something had come up with work, which was odd. Shouldn't he have been here by now?

This was the perfect time for her to freshen up and maybe see if she could get some dinner started. A nice glass of wine on the porch swing later would really top off their first night back in the home together.

Nearly an hour, a change of clothes and one casserole later, Delilah's cell chimed.

She sat the hot dish on the stovetop and removed her oven mitts before moving to the oversize kitchen island to check her cell.

I've been swamped today, babe. I won't be at the house tonight. Something has come up and I'm at the airport. Shouldn't be gone long and I'll text when I can.

Delilah stared at the words and read them over…three times.

He knew she was coming. Hell, he'd asked her to come back and stay. She told him she'd meet him here after work, but she hadn't confirmed that she'd be spending the night—she had wanted that to be a surprise.

The aroma of chicken and rice filled the kitchen, mocking her at her attempt to make this new start. She glanced down at the fitted tank dress she'd put on and figured the touch-up on makeup and hair were all for naught.

She didn't even reply. What was there to say? Night one back in the house and he already had a business trip. She'd worried he'd fall back into old patterns, but had no idea he'd choose to do them right now.

Delilah sat her cell back down and turned to the casserole. She wasn't in the mood for food anymore, but wine always seemed like the perfect idea. She chose a bottle from the wine fridge in the kitchen and gave herself a hearty pour.

Sitting on the front porch swing alone wasn't appealing anymore, so she took her glass to the bedroom. Might as well strip down and soak in a tub, because she was too tired to pack up and go back to her rental. She'd learned early on in this split that self-care was a legit need. Wine and a bubble bath would be the perfect ending to this day.

No, the perfect ending would be her husband coming home, but since that wasn't happening, she'd just have to make the best of the situation.

She couldn't help but wonder if he was even sorry for not coming home. If he even realized that he'd already slipped back into workaholic Cam when he'd vowed to put her and their marriage above all else. Did he even think of her feelings or how this would impact her at all?

The first sting of tears pricked her eyes and she blinked them away. She wasn't going to wallow in self-pity. She would relax in this bath and think about all the ways she could formulate the packages for the new brides who would want to book at the castle.

Just because her marriage was a disaster didn't mean others would be, and her clients deserved the best. She would make the most appealing package deals possible and sell their new venue offering like a champ. Delilah could and would focus on the positive—work plus Elise's wedding to Antonio would help her.

As for Camden…she didn't even know what to think anymore.

* * *

Cam's plane had just landed when his cell went off. He'd been gone two days, a day longer than expected. He'd texted and called Delilah, but she hadn't returned any of his messages. Clearly she was pissed, and rightfully so. No doubt she thought he'd deserted her, but he had a damn good explanation. He had every intention of making this up to her.

He pulled his ringing cell phone from his pocket, wondering if it was Dee finally getting back to him. But his father's name popped up and Camden sighed. Not the person he wanted to chat with right now, but he slid his finger across the screen to answer anyway.

"Dad."

"Son. Is this a bad time?"

The plane continued to taxi and Camden crossed his ankle over his knee and leaned back against the sofa.

"Just landed," he replied. "What's going on?"

"I was planning to tell you in person, but I didn't think I'd be welcome back in your home again."

Camden rubbed his hand over his forehead and thought about how he should reply to that statement.

"That would all depend on what you're wanting to say," Cam finally said. "If you and Mom plan on attacking my wife, then no, you wouldn't be welcome."

His father's heavy sigh came through the phone and there was no mistaking the frustration and, Cam thought, a little defeat. Silence filled the line and Cam leaned forward, suddenly concerned, because it wasn't like his father to hem and haw around.

"What's wrong, Dad?"

"There's no easy way to say this. Your mother and I have decided to get a divorce."

The plane came to a stop near his private hangar and Cam watched out the window on the opposite side as his SUV came into view. He'd been waiting to get home, to get back to Delilah and tell her everything that had happened.

But his world just exploded in a way he'd never, not in a million years, would have expected.

"Say something," his father demanded.

"I don't know what to say," Cam replied honestly. "Are you two serious? Or is this some tactic to get my sympathy?"

His dad didn't say anything for a moment and Camden wasn't sure how to take this, but his question was definitely justified. He wouldn't put it past his parents to stage something ridiculous for his benefit so he would push Delilah aside and focus on them. While his father had typically been a passive participant, his mother had been the louder voice in all of this. So, if anyone was going to call with some scheme, it would likely be her.

"Quite serious, Camden," his dad finally replied. "I understand why you would think this was a lie, but I assure you, we are parting ways. We've been miserable for a long time, but trying to keep up appearances for our friends and you. The longer our rift went on, the more your mother lashed out and felt she was losing you and me. I see how you are with Delilah. I understand why you've fought for what you want, and I want to say... Hell, son. I need to say I'm sorry."

Cam's pilot came from the cockpit, but Camden waved him off. This phone call was too damn important and he didn't want to miss a word of it.

The pilot opened the door and extended the steps, letting himself out. Cam would talk to him in a bit.

"You and Mom have been married for years." Cam realized he was stating the obvious, but still. This was crazy and totally unexpected. "Did you both come to this conclusion?"

"She's not happy about it, but she can't say she's surprised," his dad explained. "This has been years coming. I just realized the other night when we were at your house that you and Delilah have something real. And maybe at one time your mom and I did, too, but I don't know that we were ever happy like you two. I lost sight of everything and worried about appearances. I have to take responsibility for my actions and I'd like to apologize to Delilah, too, if you think she will let me."

Camden gripped his cell and came to his feet. "She would love that, Dad. She's only wanted to be accepted, that's all. She never asked for more."

"You've got a strong woman, Camden. She's worth fighting for."

Camden's throat clogged with emotions as he simply nodded. He knew damn well how special Delilah was. It just took her leaving for him to wake up to how he'd taken her for granted. He never meant to be that type of husband. It never even occurred to him that his grueling self-imposed schedule would conflict with his personal life. Having it all had always come second nature to him, but nothing was worth losing her. Absolutely nothing.

"If your firm would handle our case, we'd appreciate that," his father went on. "If you see that as too much of a conflict, I understand."

"No. We'll do it," Camden promised. "I'm just still processing everything."

"It's a blow, I'm fully aware. Take the time you need," his dad told him. "I'm moving into our town house in Lexington, so let me know what you need from me and how to get this going. I have no idea what the process is. Never thought I'd need a divorce attorney."

Yeah, that made two of them.

"I'll make sure the firm handles this so everything is fair for both of you," he told him. "Call me if you need me."

"I appreciate that, son. And let me know when I can come in person and apologize to Delilah."

"I will."

Camden ended the call and slid his cell back into his pocket. Raking a hand over the back of his neck, he was still rolling all this information through his head. Not only his parent's life-changing bombshell, but also these past two days. He had so much to talk to Delilah about regarding their future and he hoped she wasn't too upset that he just took off on a whim, but sometimes circumstances couldn't be helped.

As he stepped off the plane, he headed toward the hangar to find his pilot. He needed to schedule another trip, possibly two, and wanted Rob to be on standby for what might be a moment's notice.

Big things were going to happen and Camden was already anxious and excited for the rest of his life with Delilah.

Fifteen

Delilah stared at her computer and the beautiful layout she'd created for Sara to start advertising the new wedding packages on social media. But, something was missing. She couldn't quite put her finger on it, but she'd let her sisters take a peek and see what they thought.

Of course, everything could be perfectly fine and she was just in a crap mood after being alone in her house for two days. Oh, she could have returned Cam's calls or texts, or even gone back to her rental house, but she was stubborn. She was allowed that right. She would call him today if he didn't come home.

What the hell was he doing? He'd gone out of town before for work, but she always knew what was going on. He seemed so cryptic right now and the fact that he left before saying anything was irritating.

Dee sighed and reached for her coffee cup. Maybe she should have added a shot of bourbon to brighten her day, but she didn't think even Angel's Share Ten Year would perk her up at this point.

Her office door opened and closed, but she took another sip of coffee and continued to analyze the mock-up on her screen.

"I have something I need you guys to look at," she stated, assuming one of her sisters had just come in.

"I have something for you, too."

Delilah nearly spilled her coffee into her lap as she spun around at the sound of Cam's voice.

He stood right across from her desk with a folder. His hair stood on end, and T-shirt and jeans weren't typical workday attire for him. Something was off.

"Nice of you to show up," she told him, setting her mug back on her warmer. "Are you still working on those priorities?"

Maybe that was harsh. Maybe she was being bitchy, but she liked to call it cautious.

Camden offered her a smile, one that never failed to curl her toes and make her want him. Damn man always had a power over her she couldn't deny. No matter how angry or hurt she got, she clearly couldn't turn him away.

"You've been my priority since you left seven months ago," he informed her. "So, first things first."

Delilah watched as he set the folder on her desk, opened it and pulled out their divorce papers. Then he reached over to her organizer and fingered through until he found what he wanted.

He clicked the pen and Delilah's heart lurched into her throat as she continued to stare. But he made a large X over each sheet of the agreement. He slid the pen back into the holder and picked up one paper and tore it in half. Then he did the same with the next, and the next, until there was a pile of half sheets of paper.

"We're not divorcing," he told her.

"Apparently not." She leaned back in her seat, wondering what else was in that folder. "Are you ready to talk?"

"More than ready." He tapped the folder, but his dark eyes held hers. "I want you to know that no matter what you decide, I'm here."

Delilah's heart kicked up and she gripped the arms of her chair. "You're worrying me, Cam."

"There's nothing to be worried about," he assured her. "But this folder does hold some life-altering documents. When I left town, it was fast, I was hurried and there wasn't time to explain. I didn't want to say too much in case nothing came of it, but I have information for you."

Delilah eased forward, glancing at the documents beneath his hands. "About what?"

"Your father."

"What?" she whispered.

Slowly, she came to her feet, her focus going from Camden to the folder. She'd had no idea he was even looking into anything like this. He'd never said a word about it. She assumed he'd gone out of town for his own work, but he had gone for her.

"Right after you told me what you all found at Milly's house, I called my investigator." Cam flipped the top of the folder open again and pulled out a printed email. "This was his initial finding."

He handed the sheet to Delilah and she scanned it quickly, trying to take in the information all at once. Then she went back to the top and went slower. In this first look into her mother's past and her own, there was a good bit of information as to where her mother had been at that time.

In line with Sara's findings, their mother was working at a treatment facility as she was trying to get and stay clean. Then she left for about a month and came back. She wasn't back long before discovering her pregnancy. So wherever she had gone in that time, that had to have been where she met Delilah's father.

Dee pointed toward the folder. "What else?" she asked.

"You can have all of this information, but I'll give you the shortened version." Camden slid the folder across her desk. "Your mother went to Charlotte for reasons that are still unclear. Speculation is that she met someone and followed him there, but regardless, that's where your father is now. He's been there all these years. I'm not sure if he knows anything about you, but I can tell you that he's a widower and he has no children... except you."

Delilah sank back into her chair once again as she flipped through the papers. Did he want to know her? Did he want to have children? Or did he love his life the way it was?

Part of her felt a little pang of disappointment that she didn't have other siblings, but the other part knew she was blessed with the two sisters she did have.

"I saw him."

Delilah jerked her attention back to Cam. "You met him?"

"Sort of. I wanted to lay my own eyes on him." Camden shrugged and perched on the corner of her desk. "Maybe I wanted to see if you resembled him or perhaps I wanted to see how he lived his life. I just knew I couldn't come back here without telling you that I saw him."

Delilah's throat clogged with emotions and she blinked away the moisture in her eyes. "What did he look like?" she whispered.

Camden reached over and slid a photo out of the back of the folder. Delilah glanced down at a man she'd never seen in her life, but it was like looking in a mirror. The wide eyes, gentle smile and square jawline were all from her father. She'd always wondered who she looked like...now she knew.

Emotions became too much. Delilah bit down on her lip so she wouldn't start the ugly cry, but one tear fell, then another, and she couldn't stop. Camden got up and went into her adjoining bathroom, then came back out with tissues.

"Here." He handed them over and then sat on the edge of her desk beside her. "I wasn't sure how you'd take this news. I know it's a great deal to process and I didn't want you upset."

Delilah shook her head and wiped at her nose. "That's not it," she sniffed. "All of my life I've wanted to look like someone. You know? I mean, I always just said Elise and Sara were my sisters, but now we know they are. That didn't help, though, because we all are so different physically. But now I see this picture... I feel a connection to someone for the first time in my life."

She dabbed at her eyes and continued to stare at the photograph of this man.

"What's his name?" she asked.

"Luis Diaz. He's of African American, German and Puerto Rican descent. He's the owner of a coffee shop and bookstore in Charlotte."

Delilah smiled. "A business owner. Another commonality we have."

She set the picture aside and started searching through the other documents. Mostly there were printed emails and a basic background check, along with a list of Luis's parents and his siblings. There was so much material here and all of it pertained to her and her past. She'd never wanted to think too much about her past before because she didn't think it started before Milly. Never did she think any of this would come about or that Camden would go to this trouble to obtain all of these details for her.

"I'm not sure if you want to meet him or if you just wanted to have this information," Camden stated. "No matter what you decide, I'm right there with you."

Delilah shifted all the papers back into the folder and closed it, but she kept the picture out on her desk. When she glanced back up to Camden, he stared down at her with such love and care, she wasn't even sure what to say. He'd done something so amazing—he'd given her a piece of herself that she never had before.

"Honestly, I don't know what I want to do right now," she told him. "Definitely take all of this in, but I'm going to really have to think about everything. I don't want to disrupt someone's life, but at the same time I feel he deserves to know he has a child."

"You could play this from both sides all day long," Camden agreed. "You're going to have to do what's best for you and be confident in your decision."

Delilah smoothed her hair over one shoulder as she bounced around the facts she'd just been handed.

"Now I feel guilty for not returning your calls or texts." She wadded her tissues up and tossed them in the trash beneath her desk, then looked up at Camden. "I'm sorry. I assumed you went away for work and I got cranky…and apparently petty."

Cam leaned forward, turned her chair slightly so he could place his hands on the arm and cage her in. "You weren't being petty. How could you know what I was doing? Even if you'd called, I wouldn't have told you. I needed to tell you in person and I didn't want to say anything until I was positive I had all of the facts."

"I can't believe you did this," she muttered, still shocked.

"There's nothing I wouldn't do for you," he insisted. "You're above everything for me, Dee. I know I can still have a successful career, but I can also put you and us first. And you're my family now. Since marrying you, I should have started that chapter anew, but I didn't. From here on out, you are my family, and kids can be a discussion for another time. Or maybe we can just get a dog... or maybe a cat since they aren't as much maintenance. Whatever you want."

Her heart flipped as she reached up and slid her hand over his cheek. "I moved a few of my things back in."

"Is that right?" Camden took her hand and kissed her palm. "When can we go get the rest?"

"My lease is up in a few months."

"We're going to be breaking that lease," he told her. "And tell your Realtor that our house isn't for sale."

"Gladly."

He leaned down and nipped at her lips. "Is it too early for you to leave?" he murmured against her mouth.

"You can't possibly be asking me to skip work," she mocked. "Of all people, I certainly expected better from you."

Camden laughed and eased back. "Oh, that's exactly what I'm suggesting."

She looked at the computer screen with the work she'd been doing before her entire life turned upside down. She could send this to her sisters and tell them she was taking the rest of the day off with

Cam. They would understand, but even more, they would encourage this time off.

"I think I can spare the rest of the day for you," she replied.

"What about the rest of your life?"

Delilah came to her feet and stood between his legs. Looping her arms around his neck, she teased her lips against his.

"I think I can spare that, too."

Epilogue

"I don't know why I'm so nervous."

Camden leaned over and kissed her on the cheek.

"Nothing to be nervous about," he assured her. "All you have to do is be yourself."

In the week since Delilah had discovered her own father's identity, she'd been mulling over meeting him. She still hadn't decided what to do there, but today was for repairing torn relationships with Cam's family...or rather, his father.

The doorbell rang and Camden started to head toward the foyer. Delilah placed a hand on his arm.

"Let me," she told him. "He's taking a big step in coming here, so I will meet him in the middle."

Cam smiled and nodded, gesturing for her to go ahead.

Delilah took in a deep breath and went to the front door. She tucked her hair behind her ears and flicked the lock.

Cam's father stood there with flowers in hand.

"Delilah," he greeted, extending the enormous bouquet. "These are for you."

"Oh, wow. Um…thanks."

She took the flowers and turned to see Camden standing there with a smile on his face. Just that simple gesture eased her nerves.

"Come on in," she told him as she stepped aside.

The moment he was in and the door was closed, Cam's dad shook his head and spread his hands wide.

"I have no clue where to start," he began. "'I'm sorry' seems inadequate."

"'I'm sorry' is the perfect place to start," she assured him. "Just the fact you acknowledge this is a big move in the right direction."

"I told my son how lucky he was to have someone like you by his side."

Delilah couldn't help but smile. "I'd say we're both lucky. I am sorry about the divorce, though. I never wished for anyone to have heartache or be ripped apart."

"My divorce isn't your fault," he told her. "We've had problems for years, but it took seeing my son fully in love for me to realize that true love does exist. And I'm not eager to get out there and find it, but I am ready to start building my life the way I want it and putting myself first."

"I'm really happy for you, Dad."

Camden came up and gave his father a hug. Their masculine pats on each other's backs had Dee tearing up once again. This whole family comradery was seriously getting to her lately. She'd never been an emotional wreck before, but something about all of the ups and downs, losing Milly and then discovering her father had her thankful and she couldn't control her emotions.

When Camden eased back, he moved next to her and wrapped his arm around her waist.

"Are you able to stay for dinner?" Delilah asked. "We can grill something and enjoy the evening on the patio."

"I'd love to," he told her. "I feel like this is a new beginning for all of us."

Camden looked down at her and kissed her forehead.

"It definitely is," he agreed.

Delilah couldn't wait for all the possibilities to come to life. She was making amends with her father-in-law and was fairly certain she'd be reaching out to her own father. For a girl who thought she'd come from nothing, she had everything she never knew she needed right here.

* * * * *

*Don't miss the final book in the
Angel's Share trilogy*

Coming Fall 2022!

COMING NEXT MONTH FROM

DESIRE

#2899 BEST MAN RANCHER
The Carsons of Lone Rock • by Maisey Yates
Widow Shelby Sohappy isn't looking for romance, but there's something enticing about rancher Kit Carson, especially now that they're thrown together for their siblings' wedding. As one night together turns into two, can they let go of their past to embrace a future?

#2900 AN EX TO REMEMBER
Texas Cattleman's Club: Ranchers and Rivals
by Jessica Lemmon
After a fall, Aubrey Collins wakes up with amnesia—and believing her ex, rancher Vic Grandin, is her current boyfriend! The best way to help her? Play along! But when the truth comes to light, their second chance may fall apart...

#2901 HOW TO MARRY A BAD BOY
Dynasties: Tech Tycoons • by Shannon McKenna
To help launch her start-up, Eve Seaton accepts an unbelievable offer from playboy CTO Marcus Moss: his connections for her hand in marriage, which will let him keep his family company. But is this deal too good to be true?

#2902 THE COMEBACK HEIR
by Janice Maynard
Home due to tragedy, exes Felicity Vance and Wynn Oliver don't expect to see one another, but Wynn needs a caregiver for the baby niece now entrusted in his care. But when one hot night changes everything, will secrets from their past ruin it all?

#2903 THE PREGNANCY PROPOSAL
Cress Brothers • by Niobia Bryant
Career-driven Montgomery Morgan and partying playboy chef Sean Cress have one fun night together, no-strings...until they discover she's pregnant. Ever the businesswoman, she proposes a marriage deal to keep up appearances. But no amount of paperwork can hide the undeniable passion between them!

#2904 LAST CHANCE REUNION
Nights at the Mahal • by Sophia Singh Sasson
The investor who fashion designer Nisha Chawla is meeting is...her ex, Sameer Singh. He was her first love before everything went wrong, and now he's representing his family's interests. As things heat up, she must hold on to her heart *and* her business...

YOU CAN FIND MORE INFORMATION ON UPCOMING HARLEQUIN TITLES, FREE EXCERPTS AND MORE AT HARLEQUIN.COM.

HDCNM0822

*Recording studio exec Miles Woodson needs a
showstopping act for his charity talent show,
and R&B superstar Cambria Harding fits the bill.
But when long days working together become steamy
nights, can these opposites make both their passion
project and relationship work?*

Read on for a sneak peek at
What Happens After Hours
by Kianna Alexander

"There's no need to insult me, Cambria. After all, we'll
be seeing a lot of each other over the next two weeks."

"Oh, I see. You're the type that can dish it, but can't
take it. Ain't that something?" she scoffed, then shook her
head. "Let's make a deal—I'll show you the same level
of respect you show me." She grabbed her handbag from
the table. "So remember the next time you open your
mouth, you can expect me to match whatever energy you
throw out."

He watched her, silently surveying the way her glossy lips pursed into a straight line, the defiant tilt of her chin, the challenge in her eyes. She was mesmerizing, disconcerting even. No woman had ever affected him this way before. *She knocks me so off balance, but for some reason, I like it.*

Her lips parted. "Why are you staring at me like that?"

Don't miss what happens next in...
What Happens After Hours
by Kianna Alexander.

Available October 2022 wherever
Harlequin Desire books and ebooks are sold.

Harlequin.com